AGED TO PERFECTION

Book Cover Design: Jasmine Yunaa
Book Interior Design: Brady Moller

Print ISBN: 979-8-9949976-0-4
The Audacious Press

AGED TO PERFECTION

TALES FROM THE GROWN ASS WOMEN'S CLUB

FELECIA HOWELL

Contents

Acknowledgments

To ALL the Fabulous, Wise, Funny, and Sexy women who have kept me close

Thank you.

For the laughter that healed, the lessons that stuck, and the late-night check-ins that saved me.

For every truth you told over wine, over tears, over brunch, or on a random Tuesday when I needed it most.

You are my muses, my mirrors, my magic.

This book is for you.

This book is you.

With all my love,
Felecia Howell

To Gail Christian, my forever Heroine,
And to Takemi, my love & my biggest Cheerleader!
And to my mother, who simply did the best she knew how.
And, to all the Fabulous, Wise, Funny, and Sexy women who have kept me close.
To all my sistah-girlfriends, big and small, from the East Coast to the West Coast, from the big city to the desert
Y'all know who you are.
I Love You All!

The Grown Ass Women's
CLUB MANIFESTO

A declaration of laughter, truth, and unbothered joy.
We don't shrink.
We don't whisper our brilliance.
We don't apologize for becoming masterpieces.
We laugh from the gut,
love without begging,
and dance whether the music is on or not.
We carry each other, but never dead weight.
We stir stories into gumbo,
season truth with sass,
and serve it up with heels off and hearts open.
We refuse to ration joy.
Not for jobs.
Not for church folks.
Not for men with two phones.
We come back to the table again and again
messy, magical, moisturized,
with receipts in our bags and dreams on our lips.
This is our creed.
Our crown.
Our calling.

Signed,
The Founding Women of the Grown Ass Women's Club

JAZZ

CHAPTER

One

WELCOME TO THE CLUB

The night was already humming,

Soft jazz slinked through the apartment like it knew all your secrets and was saving them for a slow burn. Candles flickered on every surface, wicks dancing like they were tuned to Etta James. The living room smelled like sandalwood, old secrets, and expensive lipstick, not the fake scented kind either.

This month's gathering was at Mama Lo's place, a cozy two-story home with mismatched throw pillows, incense smoke drifting through the air, and a record player that only played albums with jazz and soul. Nina, Aretha, and Chaka had all been called to the service. No silence allowed. Only laughter, gospel truths, and enough perfume to make your head spin on an empty stomach.

Mama Lo moved with the ease of a woman who had nothing to prove. She adjusted a throw pillow with one hand and a martini in the other. Draped in a plum caftan with earrings that swayed like wind chimes, she floated around the room like the hostess of heaven itself.

Tonight wasn't just a gathering. This was a ceremony.

She whispered to the room,

"They comin', I can feel the foolishness warming up."

That's how most meetings of the Grown Ass Women's Club began. No RSVPs. No formal invitations. Just one woman's need to vent, sip, confess, or celebrate; the rest showing up with heels in hand, lashes hanging on by faith, and stories to spill like top-shelf tea.

The stemware was lined up like soldiers ready for battle, the platters arranged with olives, shrimp, and a cake that would likely get ignored until the real heat started.

She adjusted her velvet caftan, peeked at the clock, and smiled.

THE BELL RANG.

In came Miss Birdie, cane first, sparkling like disco, and zero shame, then attitude. Her hat was wide, her jacket moved like it knew the lay of the land, and her swinging pearls said she meant business. She paused just inside the doorway, surveyed the room, and announced:

"Well... the queen has arrived. Look at me! Still fine, still dangerous, and still not telling y'all where I bought this hat."

"Nice thing about being home, I don't need no hat," shot back Mama Lo.

"Do I smell butter in my pound cake?" Birdie called from the doorway, her cane tapping like a drum major in heels.

Mama Lo didn't even turn around from the stove.

"You know good and well it is," she said, flipping a towel over the cake like a prizefighter covering a champion's belt.

"You didn't use that dry mix again, did you?" Birdie asked, side-eye sharp.

Mama Lo cut her a look. "Birdie, the cake is moist. You better not start any mess before the gossip's even warm."

Birdie sauntered in, red from head to toe, and dropped her pocketbook like a mic. "If fabulous had a face, baby, well, it'd be wearing this lipstick."

She strutted past the threshold like it was a stage. The cane sparkled, and so did her grin. She made her way to her usual chair, the one with the best back support and the best view of the liquor.

Mama Lo snorted. "Sit down before your cane reports you for abuse."

DING-DONG.

Dee-Dee walked in next, bold as a protest march and just as stylish, strutting like she'd just delivered a keynote on the steps of Howard's Founders Library. Yellow HBCU sweatshirt that read "Educated AF" in rhinestones and carrying a tote bag full of bourbon and backup earrings, though she was wearing popping hoops big enough to drive through, Dee-Dee's lips were pursed like she was already mid-story.

"Make room! A legend just walked in. HBCU royalty, in the flesh! Y'all lucky I showed up. My couch was flirting with me. I know I'm late, but clearly, I brought the cute."

She tossed her coat over the chair. "I'm moisturized, educated, and two sips from spilling all the tea."

Mama Lo met her at the door, snatched the bottle, and sniffed it like a communion offering. "Whew. This'll burn something holy off your tongue."

"You're welcome," Dee-Dee said, kicking off her shoes. "I brought the one with notes of regret and just a hint of bad decisions."

"Miss Birdie!" Dee-Dee hollered. "Tell me you brought Clarice."

Birdie tapped her cane. "Clarice is always with me. Especially when I smell foolishness."

"Smells like somebody's got a testimony stewin'." Mama Lo laughed. "Only if you got the spirit to stir it. Who's ready?"

She kissed the air, slid her purse onto the bar cart, and poured herself two fingers of whiskey without looking.

ANOTHER KNOCK.

Gwen eased in slow, deliberate, dressed in leopard like a warning label. She arrived mid-phone call, cussing somebody out in fluent ex-boyfriend.

"Who ordered the mood? Because I just arrived. Don't start nothin', won't be nothin'. And y'all better compliment this leopard. I'm giving jungle and judgment tonight."

Her voice was that signature rasp. It had softened over time, soaked in gin, and still ready to bring you to your knees. It rasped like old vinyl, and when she said, "Hey babies," it sounded like both a lullaby and a dare.

She kicked off her shoes immediately.

"My feet said no, but my hips said 'Go.' So here I am."

She headed straight for the record player, gave the volume a little nudge, and hummed something sinful.

THEN CAME ZORA-LEE.

The door opened before she even knocked. Zora-Lee came in last, arms full of notebooks, cheeks already glistening with sweat. She was the newest member of the group.

"Well, look who finally found her heels and her courage," Birdie grinned while tapping her cane.

The women laughed.

"I'm not late, I'm marinated," she huffed. "This menopause is not for the weak!"

She burst in, fanning herself with a glittered hand fan and a halo of locs piled high.

Mama Lo said, "We don't do shy, baby. Not with a good bourbon and better company."

"You cute though," Dee-Dee offered, fanning her.

Zora-Lee grinned. "Still got it. Men, women, poets, don't matter. I walk in, necks turn. Y'all ain't ready for all this excellence on a weeknight!"

Wide-legged pants swishing like smoke, vintage tee, eyeliner like rebellion, and gold hoops big enough to catch secrets. She dropped to the floor in one dramatic sigh, her fan fluttering like applause.

"My uterus is trying to stage a walkout, but I told her not tonight, sis."

"Hot flash?" Gwen asked.

"If menopause had a soundtrack, it would be a fire alarm and a drumline." Dee-Dee raised her glass. "Welcome to the furnace, baby."

The others laughed.

Now that everyone had arrived, the real praise began. Compliments flew, glasses clinked, and laughter rose like incense. The air changed. It always did when the right women sat down at the same table with a little time, a little cocktail, and a lot of love between them.

Mama Lo raised her martini. "Alright now. House is full. Let's make it holy."

And every time they sat down, the rules were the same:

1. *What's said in the Club stays in the Club.*
2. *No apologies for your joy.*
3. *You must bring a drink, a truth, or a damn good story. Preferably all three.*

Tonight, they brought it all.

Gwen recounted her latest Tinder tragedy. "He said he was 6'2" but turned out to be 5'8" and spiritually unavailable. He had the nerve to bring a mixtape."

Birdie nodded solemnly. "That's grounds for tasing."

Zora-Lee raised her glass. "To mixtapes, missteps, and menopausal rage."

"To thunder thighs and thunder spirits!" Dee-Dee yelled.

Mama Lo stepped from behind the makeshift bar, swirling bourbon like it was her birthright. She lifted her glass.

"Whew! Look at this collection of sanctified trouble. My cocktail just got stronger from y'all being in the room. To another week of living, loving, and laughing like fools."

"To the Grown Ass Women's Club," Birdie said, raising her cane.

"Welcome to the Club, ladies. Let's get to free," echoed Mama Lo.

And just like that, the Club was open.

Miss Birdie crossed her legs with flair.

"Lo, you have gathered the Avengers of sass tonight."

Gwen leaned forward.

"Don't nobody light up a room like us. And don't nobody survive it better, either."

Dee-Dee smirked.

"Now can we please drink something holy before I start testifying?"

Mama Lo said with a grin, "Don't you go starting trouble before the moon gets settled."

The laughter came fast after that.

Birdie looked around and smiled. "Well look at y'all," she said. "Looking like a magazine spread on how to outlive your ex and still show up moisturized."

Mama Lo poured another round, her smile wide, knowing this was the kind of communion that didn't need wafers or wine, just women willing to tell the truth in whatever language it showed up in.

Birdie raised her glass and shouted, "To grown ass women and not needing bail money!"

Now the room erupted.

They hollered like it was revival and the Holy Ghost had just dropped it low.

Zora-Lee nodded. "I came for the wisdom and the alcohol, in that order."

"First-timers get bourbon. No exceptions," Mama Lo responded.

"So what brings you to the Grown Ass Women's Club?" Birdie asked.

Her tone was curious, but not soft.

Zora-Lee took a breath.

"I heard y'all tell stories. And I have one."

Dee-Dee grinned. "Everybody has one, baby. Question is, can yours hang?"

They all laughed again, but it wasn't mean.

It was initiation.

Zora-Lee smiled. "Only one way to find out."

There was no drum beat or ceremony. No roll call. No rules were posted.

But somehow, you knew not to interrupt.

You knew to pass the bottle without being asked.

You knew when it was your turn to listen, and when it was your time to speak.

Mama Lo raised her glass first.

"To the night."

Gwen followed.

"To the ones who made it through the last one."

Birdie lifted hers.

"To the ones who didn't, but taught us how to get here."

And Zora-Lee, clutching her bourbon with both hands, whispered:

"To whatever happens next."

"Alright, y'all," Mama Lo said, swirling her drink like a spell. "Let's start at the beginning…

Who's got a story?"

Miss Birdie cracked her knuckles. The others leaned in. The night was just heating up.

They clinked. And the stories began.

GROWN ASS HAIKU – BY Mama Lo

She stirred the silence
With a martini and a grinning
Room bowed to her fire

Warning

This book contains women who cuss, cry, and cook with soul.

Side effects may include sudden bursts of laughter, calls to old friends, cravings for pound cake, and a deep, unshakable urge to start your own Grown Ass Women's Club.

If symptoms persist?

Good.

You're doing it right.

JAZZ

CHAPTER
Two

MISS BIRDIE SPILLS IT

Birdie leaned her blinged-out cane against the side of her chair, crossed her legs, and took a long sip of her bourbon like it was holy water. She wore her signature red blazer with the rhinestone brooch shaped like a peacock and enough perfume to wake the ancestors.

"Now I'm not sayin' names," she said, eyes glinting like stained glass in candlelight, "but if any of y'all had married Leon Butterfield from down on 135th, you'd be sittin' here cross-legged and bitter too."

Dee-Dee froze mid-sip. "Leon? The one who had the lazy eye and the good credit?"

"Mmmhmm," Birdie said. "The very one who bought his mama a Lincoln but couldn't afford new drawers."

The women hollered.

Zora-Lee laughed out loud. Gwen wheezed and threw her head back like the Holy Ghost had caught her. Mama Lo had to steady her glass, already shaking from laughter.

Gwen rasped, "Birdie, you ain't got no business talkin' that slick!"

Birdie shrugged like a queen who'd been dethroned and didn't care. "I'm old, baby. I got nothin' but time, tea, and arthritis. I say what I want. Besides, I've earned this moment, and all that's going forward."

She paused, adjusted her pearls, and leaned in like a woman about to confess something especially delicious. "Now let me tell y'all how I really found out Leon was a certified, sanctified fool..."

THE REVIVAL TENT FIASCO

It was 1993. A hot, sticky Thursday evening. Birdie remembered it well because she had just gotten her rollers out and her knees greased up with Tiger Balm.

"I was wearin' my Sunday best," she said, "lookin' like deliverance with a side of don't-mess-with-me."

Leon had invited her to a revival service. Birdie thought it would be hymns and healing. Instead, it was sweat, smoke, and Sister Clarice in a mesh blouse.

"She wasn't no real sister," Birdie clarified. "She had on acrylics and the nerve to carry a tambourine in one hand and Leon's hotel key in the other."

"Whaaat," Zora-Lee gasped. Dee-Dee's eyes widened with a knowing 'this sounds like trouble coming now.' Gwen had taken off one heel and was massaging her calf like she was in labor.

"So, what'd you do?" Mama Lo asked.

"I followed 'em, like any woman with good knees and bad intentions," Birdie said. "I had on my church shoes, a belt tight enough to testify, and a bottle of hot sauce in my purse, don't ask."

"HOT SAUCE?!" Gwen and Dee-Dee said at the same time.

"Gurl, I was raised Pentecostal and petty," Birdie said. "Don't do me."

THE CONFRONTATION

Birdie waited until Leon and Sister Clarice came stumbling out the back of the tent. Clarice was laughing like the devil just told a joke. Leon looked guilty and greasy.

"I said, 'Leon Eugene Butterfield, did you bring me here to watch you fornicate in front of the Lord?!'"

Gwen choked on her drink. Dee-Dee had her head on the table. Mama Lo wheezed, "Not his middle name!"

Birdie continued without flinching. "He said, 'Birdie, it's not what it looks like!' I said, 'Then explain the lipstick, and the limp!'"

The women were hollering like it was Sunday at the Apollo.

"Where's Clarice now?" Gwen asked, trying to catch her breath.

THE CLARICE ORIGIN STORY

"You wanna know where I got this cane?" Birdie tapped it twice like it had a soul. "Clarice was born that same night."

"You mean the cane is Clarice?" Gwen blinked.

"Oh yes," Birdie nodded solemnly. "Clarice doesn't ask questions, she just shows up."

Zora-Lee clutched her chest. "You named her?"

Birdie smirked. "You name anything that protects you. She saved me from a twisted ankle and a possible murder charge."

Mama Lo held her drink like it was gospel. "This is better than television."

Gwen wiped her eyes. "You know what? I once caught my ex at a crawfish boil with a woman named Tonya who had the audacity to call me 'sis.'"

"Wait! Tonya with the eyebrows?" Dee-Dee asked.

"Yes, those brows had a whole storyline of their own!"

"See," Birdie leaned back, "we've all had a Tonya, a Leon, or a Clarice."

"And we all still look good," Mama Lo added, "so who really won?"

THE WISDOM DROP

Birdie leaned forward and tapped the table with one perfectly manicured finger. Her voice softened, just a hair.

"You know what I learned that day? Some people will pray for you in public and prey on you in private. And that's why I keep a cane, a cocktail, and a clean conscience."

The room went quiet, not because anyone felt sad, just sober. The kind of silence that says, "We've all been there."

Zora-Lee raised her glass. "To clean consciences and hot sauce."

Mama Lo shouted, "Birdie has dropped a whole sermon in here!"

"I thought I'd have to pull out my piece," Birdie added casually.

"Not a piece!" Dee-Dee said, catching her head in her hand. "Birdie, if you pull that thing out at this table, you better aim at the past!"

Birdie laughed and said, "Bless her messy heart."

GROWN ASS HAIKU – BY MISS Birdie

Some men just ain't right
Sister Clarice knows the truth
So does the cane, chile

"Who's next?" Mama Lo asked, still dabbing her eyes.

"I need another round and a fan!" Gwen pulled her straps up and winked. "I might have a little something to say!"

CHAPTER
Three

LEOPARD AND LYRICS

Gwen didn't glide into the room. No, she sauntered in, like a jazz riff with hips. Leopard print, thin straps, and that raspy laugh that always rolled in before her. She moved like she had a soundtrack playing under her skin, something with horns and heartbreak, something too sexy for radio.

"Y'all got ice?" she asked, already fishing a silver flask from her bra.

Mama Lo passed the bucket. "Always prepared, I see."

"You never know what the night is goin' require," Gwen said, pouring herself a drink. "Liquor, a good two-step, or a witness."

Dee-Dee shouted, "If you break into song, I'm throwin' a napkin and takin' my earrings off."

Zora-Lee was already mid-cackle, her fan fluttering like it had its own rhythm section ready for a fan dance.

"Oh, she gon' sing," Birdie added, settling in with a fresh pour. "She's been warming up that note since 1978."

Gwen smirked. "And it's still holdin', unlike your Spanx."

The room erupted in laughter. Gwen took a bow like she was on stage, then let out a low whistle that turned into a chuckle.

Zora-Lee leaned in, all bling and bold. "You always this smooth, Gwen? Or is this just the whiskey talkin'?"

Gwen winked. "Baby, this is years of scuffed heels and smooth jazz. The whiskey just shows up for the encore."

THE GOSPEL ACCORDING TO GWEN

Birdie raised an eyebrow. "Zora-Lee, you takin' notes or takin' names?"

"I'm takin' inventory," Zora-Lee said. "Y'all got history. I'm just tryin' to figure out how to turn my mistakes into wisdom and my exes into poems."

Gwen took a slow sip, savoring it. "Do you still got it?"

"Got what?" Zora-Lee blinked playfully.

"The nerve to show up and shine," Gwen said. "To walk into a room like it owes you applause."

Zora-Lee grinned. "I think I do. Some days, I need more fan power, but I still make heads turn… from men and women."

Dee-Dee threw both hands up. "YASS!"

They burst into another wave of laughter. Mama Lo poured a round for everybody.

"You know," she said, topping off Birdie's glass, "these nights feel like church without the guilt."

Birdie chuckled. "Speak for yourself. I came to confess and stir the pot."

GWEN'S FLASHBACK: THE MIC DROP

"Y'all ever had a moment," Gwen asked, swirling her glass, "where your body left the room, but your voice stayed?"

Mama Lo nodded. "Chile, I've had years like that."

"I was twenty-five," Gwen said. "Singing backup for a jazz band that paid me in gumbo and compliments."

Birdie muttered, "Raggedy."

"Exactly. We were at this basement lounge in Atlanta. The crowd was drunk and sticky, and my heels were half a size too small. But baby, that sax player was fine…"

"Say less," Dee-Dee grinned.

"So, the headliner gets laryngitis, and the band looks at me like, 'You ready?' I said no with my mouth and yes with my soul."

Zora-Lee leaned in, eyes wide.

"They handed me the mic," Gwen continued. "I opened with *God Bless the Child*… and before I hit the second verse, the whole place had gone still. Even the bartender stopped pouring."

Birdie whispered, "Goosebumps."

"When I finished, someone from the back yelled, 'Who raised you?!' I said, 'My grandma. And Billie Holiday.'"

GWEN'S GROWN ASS TRUTH

"I ain't famous. Never made a record. But I've been sung to, sung over, and sung through," Gwen said. "Music doesn't need a contract to make you matter. Sometimes it just needs a moment."

The room got real quiet. Not heavy. Just holy.

Dee-Dee raised her glass. "To basement gigs and gumbo paychecks."

"To standing ovations that only need four women and a drink cart," Mama Lo added.

Gwen adjusted her straps and raised her glass again.

"Don't get it twisted," she said. "I still hit notes and nerve endings."

Zora-Lee laughed. "You got a favorite?"

Gwen took a breath, let it out slow, then started to hum.

Not loud. Just low. A note that curled around the table and made the candles flicker.

Birdie closed her eyes.

Mama Lo swayed just a little.

Dee-Dee didn't interrupt.

Zora-Lee whispered, "That's it."
Gwen stopped, sipped, and smiled.
"That's enough for tonight."

GROWN ASS HAIKU – BY GWEN

Leopard and lipstick
Voice that rewrites the silence
Still singing, still soft

CHAPTER
Four

ZORA-LEE, MELANIN, METAPHORS & MOONLIGHT

Zora-Lee burst into the room like glitter and gospel. Her wide-legged pants swooshed like she was marching into her destiny, eyeliner sharp enough to cut through judgment, and locs piled into a crown of casual chaos. She wasn't always the first to speak, but tonight? "Oh, I'm ready," she said, dropping into her usual spot on the rug, cross-legged like she was at a poetry slam and the spirits were about to snap. She was more than ready to spit some truths.

"I've had three hot flashes today and a poem begging to be born," she said. Birdie leaned in, amused. "Which came first?" Zora-Lee smiled. "The sweat. Then the rage. Then the verse."

> *I walk into rooms and rearrange the air*
> *Not because I'm trying to*
> *But because somewhere between my collarbone and*
>   *my curls*
> *Lives every woman who taught me how to own space*
>   *like it's owed.*

The others looked at her with that blend of love and low-key pride. Mama Lo poured her a glass.

"She done bloomed, huh?" Dee-Dee nodded. "And she had us to water her."

"I love listening to y'all talk," Zora-Lee said. "It makes me feel less... frantic. Like maybe there's still time."

Birdie waved a hand. "Time ain't never been the issue. It's what you do with it that tells the story."

"You were always the baby," Gwen said, voice thick with fondness. "But we ain't coddle you. We let you stretch and stumble, and now look at you, ready to run the room."

"You were grown the day you walked in here quoting Audre Lorde and asking for extra olives," Birdie said.

"My mama told me that our stories are stitched into our skin. That every scar got a sound. That's why I write 'em down. I don't want to forget the music of survival," Zora-Lee grinned. "Y'all raised me with truth and cocktails. And the occasional slap on the ego."

Dee-Dee laughed. "Correction! Occasional backhand to the ego. We don't baby grown folks."

"You made me feel seen," Zora-Lee said softly. "Even when I was still figuring out what parts of me were worthy of showing."

Gwen nodded, her voice thick with fondness. "That's 'cause we don't do half-woman energy in this house. You either bring your whole self or you get the porch."

Zora-Lee raised her glass. "Well, I appreciate it. Even if some of y'all got me cryin' in the bathroom sometimes."

Birdie sipped. "Gurl, if you ain't shed tears over one of Mama Lo's speeches or Gwen's songs, you ain't really been loved yet."

She looked at the women, one by one. "Y'all ever feel like you spent so much time surviving, you forgot to sing?" Gwen raised her glass in silence.

Zora-Lee took a deep breath. "I used to perform in parks, on stoops, on stages built from stolen milk crates. And people would say, 'You so strong, sis.' And I'd nod like it was a compliment. But what I wanted to say was, 'I'm tired, baby. I don't want to be strong. I want to be held.'"

Birdie whispered, "Preach."

Zora-Lee stood, barefoot now, her pants loosening and swaying like passing breeze. And with a quiet confidence, she spoke the poem that had been pressing against her bones all day…

POEM: "THE SOUND OF MY NAME" – BY ZORA-LEE

> I have bled in daylight
> And smiled through it.
> Carried silence like satin,
> Made mourning into rhythm.
> They called me strong
> I called me tired.
> But I still showed up
> In every room
> As my whole damn self.
> Don't you dare forget
> That Black women
> Invented thunder
> While Silence fell

The table sat in silence for a beat too long, then Mama Lo clapped, one solid time, and the rest followed. They didn't shout. They didn't holler. They just rose up inside.

Birdie reached for the napkins. Gwen sighed, "Now see, my mascara ain't waterproof."

Dee-Dee poured another round. "Somebody pass me a fan and a therapist."

Zora-Lee laughed through her tears. "I'm just sayin' what I know."

Mama Lo raised her glass. "Then say it again, baby."

And just like that, the circle breathed deeper.

A little later that evening, when the glasses hinted for a refill and stories were ready for more rounds, a younger woman, maybe a niece, maybe a neighbor, maybe just a soul in need, knocked softly on the door.

She stepped in, shy and unsure, cradling a small notebook.

"I heard y'all tellin' stories," she said quietly. "I write too... but I don't think I'm ready."

Zora-Lee walked right over and took the girl's hands in hers.

"You don't have to be ready," she said. "You just have to be real. Ready is for people who think stories need permission."

The girl blinked. "But I'm scared I'll mess up."

Zora-Lee smiled. "Baby, we all mess up. That's why Miss Birdie carries a cane named Clarice."

"Excuse me?" the girl giggled.

"She uses it to poke people who forget who they are."

Birdie, slow nodding with her drink in hand, didn't even look up. "And it's polished and petty just like me."

The girl laughed. "Can I come back next time?"

Zora-Lee looked around the room. Every woman nodded.

"Long as you bring a truth and a snack," Dee-Dee said.

"Preferably something fried," Gwen added.

"And before Grown AF hour!" shouted Birdie.

There was laughter all around. And just like that, another seat at the circle was claimed.

POEM: "WHAT CATCHES FIRE" – BY ZORA-LEE

I used to beg for sparks, tiny flickers of maybe. Tried to build bonfires out of borrowed matches and gaslighting smiles. But then Y'all showed up. With candles and cackles, gasoline truths, and fans full of fight. You didn't rescue me. You re-lit me. **And** now everything I touch catches fire.

GROWN ASS HAIKU – BY ZORA-LEE

Lit the wrong candle
Still rose, still wrote, still radiant
Ashes make good ink

Mama Lo slid a dish of spiced nuts toward her. "Have a snack, baby. Wisdom is heavy. You gotta chew between bites."

The room hummed with a warmth that settled deep. This was more than a gathering, it was a passing of soul, sip by sip.

Birdie sat up straighter. "Now who brought the good gossip?"

Zora-Lee leaned back, eyes twinkling. "Lawd Miss Birdie."

Birdie grinned. "Say my name, say my name!"

And just like that, the torch was lit, and the night caught fire again.

Zora-Lee wasn't done.

"I was at the bus stop the other day, and this baby girl couldn't have been more than twenty, looked at me and said, 'How do you move like you own everything?'"

The women leaned in.

Zora-Lee smiled. "I told her, 'Because I stopped asking for permission to shine.' And then I wrote this."

POEM: "THIS FLAME DON'T FOLD" – BY ZORA-LEE

They asked me to be water, I gave them fire. Asked me to be quiet, I sang louder in the choir. Said sit down, I danced. Said smile pretty, I laughed with my whole damn chest. I am not your soft apology. I am your spark. Your Sunday shout. I am the flame That don't fold.

Gwen raised her glass. "Girl. That was a sermon and a strut."

Dee-Dee shouted, "I'm bout to get that on a mug and a church fan!"

Miss Birdie shook her head. "See? I would've said all that too but I'd get winded climbing the church steps."

Zora-Lee laughed, pointing. "And didn't you almost take somebody out with your cane?"

Birdie tapped her cane on the floor. "Clarice don't play. She got aim and arthritis."

They burst out laughing again.

Mama Lo raised her glass one last time. "To the baby of the bunch. Who ain't no baby anymore."

Zora-Lee, smiling through her tears, whispered, "Thank you for seeing me."

GROWN ASS HAIKU – BY ZORA-LEE

They spoke, and I bloomed
I caught fire, then I flew
Still dancing barefoot

CHAPTER
Five

HIGHER LEARNING, LOWER PATIENCE

By this point in the night, the air was thick with truth, lies, and leftover lipstick on cocktail rims, Mama Lo had gone into the back of the cabinet like she was unlocking a vault.

And then…

The bottle hit the table like it had its own entrance music.

This was Uncle Melvin's WooBaby Private Reserve. The label was hand-drawn, half-peeled, and loud:

"UNCLE MELVIN'S PRIVATE RESERVE, WOOO BABY!, DRINK AT YO' OWN RISK."

"Now y'all be careful," Mama Lo said, eyes wide and smiling the way only someone who knows better smiles. "Uncle Melvin didn't make this for the weak of will or bladder."

"Here comes the good stuff!" Dee-Dee announced, holding it up like a holy relic.

Birdie crossed herself and muttered, "Lord Jesus."

Gwen leaned over the table and whispered, "Gurl, we 'bout to go there? Oh, we about to raise the roof now!"

"We don't need to turn down, for what?!" Zora-Lee said, feeling grown.

Mama Lo poured it neat. No ice.

Dee-Dee picked up the bottle, sniffed it, and immediately pulled back like it had slapped her spirit. "This smells like it's aged in vengeance and baptisms. Please don't add any fire to this!"

"WooBABY!" Dee-Dee croaked after her first sip. "What is this, raised in a gospel choir and set in betrayal?"

Mama Lo poured the shots generously, glowing pours that shimmered with danger. Then she raised her glass and said, "Ladies… may your wigs stay on and your truths come out."

They were gone after that.

And Mama Lo? She just sat back, smug and smirk-like. She too was glowing, watching a storm she'd predicted roll in right on schedule.

Gwen was humming *Ain't No Way* like she was back in love with her fourth ex.

Birdie was fanning herself with her church fan, the one with MLK on one side and the funeral home info on the back.

Zora-Lee had her legs curled beneath her, her fan beating time like she was directing a jazz band.

That's when Dee-Dee slammed her glass on the table like a gavel. She stood mighty with all her 'Educated AF' five-foot-four frame. To have her tell it, though, she was always six feet.

"Alright. I got one."

The room hushed. Well, as hushed as five tipsy women can get.

"I was once proposed to by a Nigerian prince," she said, deadpan.

Zora-Lee coughed on her drink. "A real prince or one of them 'send me your account info' princes?"

"He had a compound, a driver, and two wives already," Dee-Dee said. "Told me I'd be the American Empress."

Mama Lo sipped slow. "You sure he didn't mean his American Express? That ain't a proposal, baby, that's a time-share."

The women laughed. Gwen nearly knocked over the Uncle Melvin bottle. Miss Birdie stomped her cane like she was calling down judgment.

"But the man was fine," Dee-Dee added. "Had shoulders like he chopped wood with intention."

"You lyin'," Gwen choked.

"I am," Dee-Dee confessed. "But it's a good lie."

By this point, the Private Reserve had everybody a little louder, a little looser, and a lot more reckless with the truth.

But Dee-Dee wasn't done. She grinned and said, "He offered me gold and two acres of land. Said he'd throw in a goat with blue eyes to sweeten the deal."

Gwen's drink nearly came out of her nose. "Now, gurl, you know you lyin'!"

The women fell out.

Then Mama Lo, eyes twinkling, said, "Alright now, if we're tellin' tales, let me remind y'all about the time Miss Birdie ran from a state trooper on foot and got away."

Miss Birdie sat up tall. "I did not run. I moved strategically. There's a difference!"

They all hollered with laughter, jostled, gasped for air, clutching wigs, leaning on shoulders, and begging for breath. The room was shaking with joy and bad decisions.

"I swear this night should be illegal," Gwen said. "We need to film this and sell it as therapy."

Mama Lo waved her hand. "Gurl, you need to write this mess down."

"I do!" Zora-Lee shouted. "I need a whole anthology of Dee-Dee's Disappointments!"

Dee-Dee raised a brow. "Excuse you! It's called growth, thank you very much."

Then she got that look, the one she got before she took folks to school.

"You know," she said, leaning back, "some folks think wisdom comes in silence. But I learned mine at the card table."

"Bid Whist or Spades?" Birdie asked, already knowing.

Mama Lo chuckled. "Here she goes. She's warmed up now."

Dee-Dee leaned in. "Now y'all know I went to The Mecca. That's right, Howard University. I remember sitting on the quad with a deck of cards in one hand and a protest sign in the other."

Zora-Lee grinned. "You stayed ready."

"Always," Dee-Dee said. "One day, we were in the middle of a Bid Whist tournament when the admin tried to sneak in some nonsense policy about 'curfew enforcement.'"

Gwen let out a wheeze. "Curfew? On Black excellence?!"

"Exactly," Dee-Dee said, slapping the table. "So we threw our cards down, marched straight to the Dean's office, and occupied it until 3 a.m."

"Was it successful?" Mama Lo asked.

"Hell yes," Dee-Dee said. "By morning, we had a DJ who loved *go-go* music, snacks, and a full-on sleep-in. The Dean ended up joining us. Said he heard Chuck Brown and knew the situation was real."

"Whist, baby. The table was sacred. I came up in dorm rooms and protest marches. Howard University, mid-eighties. We were loud, we were bold, we were cute and correct. I wore hoop earrings with a purpose and lipstick that said, 'step back.'"

Gwen nodded. "Say that."

"One night, we were marching against tuition hikes by day and flipping cards in our dorm lobby by night. Then here came the Dean again; he walked in during our tournament and tried to shut it down. Said it was disrupting order."

"What happened?" Zora-Lee asked.

Dee-Dee sipped. "We dealt him in. He played a mean hand, too. That man reneged once and blamed it on the system."

Mama Lo laughed so hard she wheezed. "Not the Dean blaming institutional failure on a card game!"

"I'm tellin' you," Dee-Dee said, "Black joy is resistance. Ain't nothing more revolutionary than laughing, playing, and refusing to let the world wear you down."

Birdie clinked her glass. "A-freakin'-men."

Dee-Dee took another sip. "I don't mess around. These days, the only thing I protest is weak drinks and people who ask, 'Was Howard really that special?'"

Zora-Lee tilted her head. "What do you say?"

"I say, 'You see this sweatshirt, baby?' Then I raise my glass, quote Audre Lorde, and keep it pushing."

"You always had that fire," Miss Birdie said with a proud nod.

"It ain't gone," Dee-Dee replied. "I just drink better whiskey now."

"Hear, hear," the women raised their glasses in unison.

Then Gwen whispered, "Didn't you once date that poet who only spoke in haikus?"

Dee-Dee groaned. "Ugh. That man couldn't count syllables or keep a job."

They collapsed with laughter.

"I tried to be patient," Dee-Dee said. "But after the third 'rose petal soul, I'm whole' mess he sent me, I said, 'Sir, this is not therapy. It's Thursday.'"

Zora-Lee screamed. "He said 'I'm whole'? Was he even paying rent?!"

"Nope. But he said he paid in spirit."

Birdie stood up with her cane. "I'm calling the ancestors. We need backup."

By the end of the story, Dee-Dee was fanning herself with a napkin and humming the Howard fight song. Miss Birdie was threatening to take everybody to church, and Gwen was trying to remember if she still had that fringe dress that got her locked in the closet of a green room.

Mama Lo took another sip, looked around the room, and said, "Chile, this ain't just a party. This is testimony in high heels."

And they all raised their glasses again, ready for whatever came next.

Dee-Dee slapped the table and declared:

"From this day forward, I reserve the right to edit my own life story for dramatic effect and spiritual accuracy."

And with that, she raised her glass for a toast.

GROWN ASS HAIKU – BY DEE-DEE DON'T

Fact-check my tale
Ain't no lies, just lived with flair
Truth wears lipstick too

As they refilled glasses and resumed the chaos, Mama Lo whispered, "Now this is a healing circle."

Birdie added, "With a splash of foolish."

Gwen leaned back, grinning. "And a shot of WoooBaby for good measure."

The roof didn't just raise, it remembered.

The laughter became a wave. Now the tears were dropping from laughing so hard, Gwen was on the floor, fanning herself, and Birdie was halfway into her third shot.

Even the plants seemed to sway in sympathy.

That bottle made stories start flowing like praise at a revival. And it wasn't long before someone said…

"Alright y'all… who's next to tell a tale?"

GROWN ASS HAIKU – BY MISS Birdie

Sip of Uncle's sin
Now I'm confessing to crimes
And I look damn good

CHAPTER
Six

I'M FINE, MY ASS

Mama Lo poured another round, sliding the bottle across the table like a secret.

"I don't care what anybody says," she began, "the biggest lie Black women ever told was, 'I'm fine.'"

That stopped the room.

Zora-Lee let out a slow, "Whew…"

Birdie clutched her pearls dramatically, since she was the only one wearing them, and said, "Lo, you 'bout to make me call my therapist and my ex in the same breath."

Dee-Dee leaned forward. "Ain't that the truth. I've been 'fine' through marriages, miscarriages, bad wigs, layoffs, and my second knee."

Gwen nodded. "Chile, I was 'fine' the day I left Jerome… and the day I found out he left his saxophone behind. Took me six years to realize I wasn't fine, I was free."

The room went still in the best way; quiet enough to feel safe, loud enough to echo.

Mama Lo sipped her drink and let it hang.

"We say it because we have to," she said. "Because we raised everybody else. Because if we fall apart, who's gonna hold the pieces?"

Birdie crossed her legs with a grunt and tilted her glass toward the ceiling. "We be 'fine' with full grocery bags and busted backs. Fine with cracked heels and cracked hearts. Fine while planning a funeral and a potluck in the same damn hour."

Gwen let out a raspy, "Mmm-hmm."

Dee-Dee raised a hand like she was testifying in somebody's Baptist church. "Don't let the lashes fool you. I cried in a Walgreens parking lot last Tuesday… with a full face of Fenty."

Zora-Lee gasped. "Not Fenty!"

"Yes, baby. And that lip stayed PUT."

The room cackled, the kind of laugh that pushed back grief.

Zora-Lee wiped the corner of her eye. "I feel like y'all are telling me how to grow old with style and survive with soul."

Mama Lo turned to her, lips soft but sharp.

"No, baby. We telling you how to do both and laugh so loud they hear you in heaven."

Gwen sat up, swirling her glass.

"You know what I hate most about 'I'm fine'? It doesn't let nobody help you. You say it too many times, and people stop asking. I say, hell to not bein' fine."

Then, something shifted.

Birdie pulled Clarice close and said, "I used to think silence was strength."

Mama Lo shook her head. "Silence is a recipe for ulcers and bad poetry."

"I thought if I broke, I'd be useless," Zora-Lee said softly.

Dee-Dee reached across the table and touched her hand. "Baby, every masterpiece has cracks. That's how the light gets in."

A moment passed. Just breath and blinking and the quiet hum of women who know things now.

Then Gwen, always the mood-flipper, said, "But y'all are aware I cussed out my chiropractor last week because he said my posture was defensive?"

"You are defensive," Birdie said.

"I'm a Black woman in America. I got a license for it."

Birdie raised an eyebrow. "Well, that explains half my last relationship."

"To not hiding it anymore," said Dee-Dee.

Zora-Lee whispered, "To truth."

Zora-Lee shook her head. "So what do we say instead?"

Mama Lo answered without missing a beat:

"Tell the truth. Or at least tell the real lie. Say, 'I'm unraveling but still moisturized.'"

Dee-Dee snapped her fingers. "Say, 'I cried in the car but my lashes held.'"

Birdie nodded. "'I'm blessed but on probation.'"

Zora-Lee whispered, "To truth."

Gwen raised her glass. "'I'm holy but don't test me.'"

Zora-Lee chuckled softly.

They clinked glasses like a choir taking communion, and for a moment, just a moment, the room didn't need music.

They were the harmony.

GROWN ASS HAIKU

> *Smile wide, shoulders tight*
> *"I'm fine" stitched into my spine*
> *Sometimes, I just get tired*

COCKTAIL CARD: "I'M FINE, MY ASS"

Ingredients:

- **2 oz. bourbon** (for the pain you ignored)
- **1 oz. sweet vermouth** (for the sweetness you gave everyone but yourself)
- **A dash of bitters** (because… life)
- **An orange twist** (for style, not apologies)

Instructions:

Pour over ice. Sip slowly, cry if needed. Cackle after, repeat with friends who call you by your whole damn name.

Seven

MISS BIRDIE, A CANE, A SECRET, AND A WHOLE LOTTA TRUTH

Clarice hit the floor before Miss Birdie said a word, tap. (Punctuation.) Tap-tap. (Pay attention.) By the third tap, even Uncle Melvin stood still.

The room went silent, and the ladies sat up straight, well, as straight as they could muster at this point in the evening.

Birdie didn't sit down; she landed in that chair like a one-woman parade. Red hat cocked like gossip. Pearls double-knotted like a threat, swinging like wind chimes in a thunderstorm. Lipstick? A whole threat.

That cane sparkled in the light. It glittered like it had seen things, and blackmailed them all. Secrets engraved in rhinestones.

"Y'all ever carry somethin' around so long," she began, "that it starts carrying you?"

Zora-Lee leaned forward like it was story time at the grown folks' table and a sermon at the same time. Gwen grabbed another shot of Uncle Melvin's. Dee-Dee crossed her legs and muttered, "Oh Lord, let me brace myself." Birdie smiled wide and wicked.

"Now I know y'all think Clarice here is just decoration." She lifted her cane and tapped the handle with one perfectly manicured finger.

"Wrong. This girl's been with me longer than some of y'all been wearing bras that fit, and that's saying somethin', Lo."

Mama Lo raised an eyebrow but said nothing. Her drink said plenty. The laughter was immediate.

"She don't just help me walk," Birdie continued. "She keeps my secrets, and my balance, especially after two martinis."

Then she leaned in, voice dropping like it was classified.

"That cane's been in bar fights, baptisms, two bachelorette weekends, and one Vegas hotel room I will not discuss due to legal reasons, a restraining order, and an expired passport."

The room exploded with laughter.

Dee-Dee shouted, "NOT the passport!" Zora-Lee was already taking notes. Birdie twirled it once with wrist action that made Gwen whistle, then tapped again.

"But tonight," she said, voice softening, "I'm gonna tell y'all what I put inside it."

Dee-Dee nearly spilled her drink. "INSIDE?! It's hollow?!"

Birdie grinned. "Baby, this ain't just a cane. It's a Black woman's emergency kit, it's a crisis management system."

She stood up slowly, slow enough to build suspense, then clicked something near the handle and revealed something tiny and unknown.

Out popped a hidden compartment, slick as sin. Inside:

- **A folded $50 bill**
- **A matchbook from a jazz club in Harlem**
- **A single gold hoop earring** ("leftover from a good night")
- **A mini flask engraved with:** *Trust No Man After Midnight*
- **And a peppermint from 1987, still perfectly wrapped, "for communion emergencies"**

Gwen clutched her chest. Zora-Lee gasped. "That's the most beautiful thing I've ever seen."

Birdie sat back down with a sigh that was half memory, half satisfaction.

"I used to carry shame. Now? I carry receipts and hydration."

She sipped, then tossed out the bomb:

"I carried my secrets like they were shame," she said. "Until one day, I realized I was confusing 'private' with 'buried.'" She paused and leaned forward just enough to cause a stir in her pearls.

"I may or may not have hosted a poker night in the church basement for… oh, four years."

Dee-Dee choked on her drink. "May or may not?!"

"We funded two scholarships and a new water heater. And new communion trays," Birdie said, head high with pride. "The deacon found out and asked to deal the next hand."

The women lost it. Dee-Dee slid to the floor. Gwen slapped the table so hard even WooBaby jumped.

"You criminal," Gwen wheezed.

"I'm a woman," Birdie replied, smoothing her pants. "With bills and an excellent poker face. I told y'all," she said, reapplying her lipstick, "I'm anointed… just not licensed."

Mama Lo had to take her glasses off to wipe her tears. "Birdie, you're gonna send me to glory early."

As the laughter died down, Zora-Lee wiped her eyes.

"What changed? Why tell it now?"

Birdie looked at her cane, then the circle of women, then the flame of the nearest candle.

"I'm not taking my brilliance to the grave so the church ladies can act surprised at my funeral. Because if I go, and y'all let the church ladies pretend I was boring, I will haunt your breakfast biscuits."

She raised Clarice like a sword and royalty, all in one.

"She's held my sass, my sins, my survival, and one emergency earring. And now? She's held by y'all too."

Dee-Dee raised her glass. "To the Queen of the Cane."

Just one clink. One breath. One moment of collective memory.

Zora-Lee added a haiku on a napkin:

Baptized in boldness
Birdie and her blinged-out truth
Clarice, though shiny, don't play fair

CHAPTER
Eight

SECRETS, PANTYLINES & "THE FLORIDA SITUATION"

The evening had crossed into that sacred pocket of time. It was the hour when the night loosened its grip and the room exhaled; no rushing, no performing, just women settling into themselves.

Zora-Lee had settled into a fuzzy throw pillow like she was melting into memory foam.

Gwen had her leopard-print heels off and one leg flung across a stool.

Miss Birdie was sipping Uncle Melvin's Private Reserve like holy water,

and Dee-Dee was already side-eyeing her second shot.

That's when Mama Lo cleared her throat and said,

"So… are we going to talk about The Florida Situation or not?"

The room went quiet, like somebody unplugged the jazz.

Mama Lo continued,

"Well, Birdie, you gonna tell that child about our road trip, or should I do the honors?"

"Oh Lord," Gwen murmured. "I thought we left that in 1994."

"Girl, please," said Birdie. "I still got sand in my shoes and trauma in my spirit."

Zora-Lee's eyes lit up.

"What Florida Situation?"

They all looked at each other like somebody needed to tell it, but nobody wanted to go first.

Dee-Dee broke.

"Fine. But this is off the record, Zora. You put one syllable of this in a poem; I'm cutting off your dreadlocks and making a protest sign."

"Deal," Zora-Lee said, grabbing her cocktail like a journalist holding a recorder.

"Now tell it slow, so I can savor every lie."

"It started with a women's empowerment weekend in Tampa," Mama Lo began.

"Y'all remember that? Back when we were still wearing high-waisted linen and shoulder pads."

"And wigs with too much attitude," Birdie added, tapping her own natural curls.

"Anyway," Gwen said, shaking her head,

"we all went thinking it was going to be workshops and affirmations.

Instead, we ended up in a strip club, a fish fry, and a police station. In that order."

"What?! A strip club?" Zora-Lee's mouth dropped open.

"Place was called Blessed & Barely Covered," said Gwen.

"We only went in 'cause the flyer said 'Free fish plate with drink purchase.'"

"That sounds like a ministry and a mistake," Zora-Lee replied.

"Oh, it was," said Mama Lo. "But that catfish?"

Gwen nodded solemnly. "Yup. Served out the back by a woman named Miss Nita, who called everybody 'sugar' and wore ankle weights while she cooked."

Birdie grinned, eyes closed like she was tasting the memory.

"That hush puppy nearly made me moan."

Dee-Dee fanned herself. "I still don't know if I was crying from joy or the hot sauce."

Birdie sipped, eyes gleaming.

"Then there was that man... That man with the snakeskin boots and a gold tooth told me he was a retired deacon.

How was I supposed to know he ran an illegal bingo hall out of the back of his trailer?"

"Oh sweet Jesus," Dee-Dee covered her face, laughing.

"He said his name was Minister Mellow, Birdie," Gwen said, waving her hand.

"That's right!" Birdie shouted.

"And he was mellow! Until the lights went out and he ran out the back with somebody's handbag and a cooler full of Hennessy."

The room erupted.

"Miss Birdie, you didn't!" Zora-Lee was on her knees, cracking up.

"I chased him!" Birdie yelled, slapping her thigh.

"In a wedge heel! Almost caught him too."

"And I got it on VHS, baby!" Mama Lo raised her glass, tears in her eyes.

"True story," Dee-Dee held up her hand.

"When the cops came, we all pretended we didn't know her.

I said my name was Denise and I was from Seattle."

"You dirty!" Birdie pointed her cane.

"You ain't even blinked twice. Just left me out there like a stray poodle with a glitter bra and one eyelash hanging!"

They laughed so hard Gwen had to lean on the table.

"The strip club had no windows," Dee-Dee gasped,

"a velvet Jesus in the corner, and a pole so greasy I swear one of the dancers slid into another tax bracket mid-spin."

"A velvet Jesus?" Zora-Lee gasped.

"This is better than anything on Netflix."

Birdie wheezed.

"I followed Leon Butterfield and Sister Clarice from the revival tent once,, I wasn't scared then!"

"Birdie, focus," Mama Lo warned through laughter.

"You were the one shouting in the holding room."

"Wait, y'all got arrested?!" Zora-Lee gasped.

Birdie looked at her sideways.

"Oh baby… that wasn't even the wildest part."

"Somebody," Mama Lo interrupted,

"lost their drawers in the parking lot."

The silence hit like thunder.

Then Birdie, Dee-Dee, and Gwen all pointed at each other at the same time.

"LIES!" Dee-Dee hollered.

"Y'ALL DON'T KNOW MY LIFE!"

The room exploded again, napkins thrown, drinks spilled, Gwen shaking her head, whispering,

"I swear I don't know how we made it out of our forties alive."

"And when we got to the police station," Mama Lo said,

"they put us all in this little back room that smelled like sweat and regret, and said,

'Ma'ams, are y'all in some kinda senior prank club?'"

"That fool cop asked if we were an all-girl band!" Birdie hollered.

"What did you say, Mama Lo?!" Zora-Lee was doubled over.

"I told him we were on a church retreat gone wrong and started praying in tongues right there in the room!"

"Birdie was shouting, Dee-Dee was singing *Take Me to the King*, and I was doing the Electric Slide, trying to distract the rookie!"

Zora-Lee was howling.

"Y'all are RIDICULOUS!"

Birdie wiped her eyes, breathless.

"But baby… we got out. No bail. No fingerprints.

Just sore feet, greasy bags of fish, and one less set of drawers between us."

Mama Lo raised her glass like a victory flag.

"To the Florida Situation, where we lost our dignity but kept our damn sisterhood!"

They laughed through the lies,
held each other up with the truth.
Wedges and wisdom.
And just like that, they all toasted.
Not because they were proud of what happened
but because they were proud, they could still tell it,
with bellies shaking and hearts full.
They hollered like it happened yesterday.
And maybe, in some sweet magical way,
it always would.

GROWN ASS HAIKU – BY ZORA-LEE

Velvet Jesus watched
Hush puppies, cuffs, laughter loud
In truth, we survived in heels

JAZZ

CHAPTER
Nine

THE NIGHT EVERYONE DANCED
ANYWAY WITH UNCLE MELVIN

Featuring: Everybody (yes, everybody)

Nobody even knows who brought the bottle of moonshine, it showed up on the bar between the shrimp cocktail and the deviled eggs like it had RSVP'd with the ancestors and arrived fashionably late.

The label said:

"Uncle Melvin's Private Reserve, DRINK AT YO' OWN RISK"

and had a drawing of a mule falling down.

Mama Lo had it locked up in her bar from God knows when.

Miss Birdie took one sniff and declared,

"That ain't liquor, that's a lawsuit."

But Dee-Dee?

She poured two fingers and said,

"If I die, put this on my tombstone: She went out glowing and giggling."

It started like any other First Friday:

Shoes too high, lashes too long, secrets too juicy.

Zora-Lee brought a new poem.

Gwen was humming something low and bluesy.

Mama Lo had on earrings shaped like tiny martini glasses that clinked when she blinked.

Then Tina showed up.

Tina was Mama Lo's cousin "from the 'burbs."

She came in hot, wearing a Fashion Nova catsuit, a leopard trench (Gwen squinted suspiciously), and a clutch shaped like a microphone.

She also brought a Bluetooth speaker and her own playlist titled:

"GROWN ASS ANTHEMS (EXPLICIT VERSION)."

"Y'all don't mind if I add a little… spice, do you?" she said, already connecting the speaker, Gwen whispered,

"Lord, she looks like somebody who throws hands at baby showers."

Mama Lo just said,

"This is about to get ignorant."

The beat dropped.

Tina hit the dance floor first, doing moves that should've come with a chiropractor on standby.

Zora-Lee tried to follow but slipped off her wedge and nearly rewrote her will on the floor.

"Someone catch that child!" Dee-Dee hollered.

Miss Birdie, halfway through her second mystery cocktail, just hollered,

"Let her learn!"

And then it happened.

Gwen, who hadn't danced since the Obama administration,

stood up, cracked her neck, and did The Rockaway with so much sass,

somebody called their ex just to apologize.

Wigs shifted.

Lashes lifted.

Mama Lo's false eyelash flew across the room and landed on a deviled egg.

Tina toasted to "freedom and footwork."

The moonshine started a side effect no one was ready for, truth-telling.

- **"I slept with a man for his ribs once!"** Dee-Dee shouted.
- **"I used to tell people I was vegan to avoid cooking!"** Zora-Lee yelled.
- **"I have two pensions and never told my third husband. May he rest... confused."** Miss Birdie slurred.

By the end of the night:

Gwen was slow-dancing with a chair; someone started a conga line that led to the bathroom.

Mama Lo stood on a stool yelling:

"This ain't menopause, this is the revival!"

Eventually, the music stopped, not because they were tired.

Oh no, sugar, but because the Bluetooth speaker died mid-twerk, and nobody could figure out how to reset it.

Zora-Lee blamed Mercury in retrograde.

So, they danced anyway.

No music. No beat, just heartbeats, belly laughs, and the creak of knees refusing to cooperate, and somehow, that was the best part.

Later, as Mama Lo sipped water and rubbed her ankles,

she whispered to no one in particular,

"Whew, I'm gonna feel this in the morning... but baby, tonight was worth it."

Tina hollered,

"Well, I've done my part, peace out!"

She collected her dead Bluetooth and was out the door.

GROWN ASS HAIKU – BY ZORA-LEE

Nothing but the brown truth
Slick shoes, two hips, and a wink
Nobody sat down

CHAPTER
Ten

PANTYHOSE & PAYBACK

(Another Reminisce)
Starring Miss Birdie and Mama Lo

Mama Lo adjusted her hat in the rearview mirror, wide-brimmed. Black. Blessed.

"This is not how I planned my Saturday," she said.

Miss Birdie, riding shotgun, was smoothing down her pantyhose with one hand and loading her purse with peppermint, a church fan, and what looked suspiciously like a taser with the other.

"Lo, we going to war. You don't plan protests, you prepare for 'em."

They were headed back to their old stomping ground: the Church Hill Community Center.

The place that raised half the neighborhood's children, hosted every fish fry, voter registration, and jazz night since 1965.

Now, some shiny-suit developer wanted to knock it down and put up a luxury high-rise and a dog spa.

Birdie squinted at the glossy print flyer in hand and read it out loud, one eyebrow already in mid-air:

"Coming Soon: The Mint Luxury Condos, Wellness Lounge and Pet Spay."

"Not on my watch," Birdie said, her pearls rattling with purpose.

"Dogs don't need saunas. People need somewhere to teach their kids how to double-dutch."

Birdie grunted.

"We used to play gin rummy in that basement. That's where your cousin met his third wife."

"And his parole officer," Mama Lo added.

They looked at each other.

No words.

Just a shared expression that meant:

They had messed with the wrong aunties today.

They pulled up to the center in full battle gear:

- Birdie in her protest boots and a caftan that read: "Not Today, Gentrification."
- Mama Lo in a power suit and earrings that clacked like judgment.
- Birdie: cane in one hand, a folding chair in the other.
- Mama Lo: pearls, pinstripe blazer, and a t-shirt underneath that read: "No Justice, No Jazzercise."

"You bring the sign?" Lo asked.

Birdie reached into the back seat and held up a cardboard masterpiece:

"Pantyhose Tight, Morals Tighter – Save Church Hill!"

They marched up the city steps.

Inside the city planning meeting, they took their seats, third row, dead center.

The developer, looking young, shiny, and suspiciously smooth, was giving a presentation packed with buzzwords like "revitalization" and "vibrancy."

"We know what that means," Birdie whispered.

"Yep. Gentrify, rebrand, and kick the history out the back door."

They didn't say anything, yet.

But when the developer showed a mockup that replaced their beloved center with a yoga deck and juice bar called Beet + Vibe, Mama Lo's hand shot up.

"Excuse me. Where exactly are the elders supposed to stretch their arthritis and play bingo now?"

"We'll have inclusive programming," he said.

Birdie stood.

"You mean the jazz class taught by that robot instructor? We read the agenda."

Gasps.

"We aren't done," Mama Lo said, in that tone that made deacons sit straighter.

"Uh, ma'am, I don't think..." the developer began.

"That's right. You don't," Birdie interrupted. "Now listen up."

Within minutes, a small crowd of old neighbors and curious looky-loos had gathered.

Miss Birdie launched into a full sermon.

Then came the real chaos.

Mama Lo pulled out a folded paper titled:

"Top Ten Reasons Why This Project Is Rude, Reckless, and Anti-Black."

She read each one with a pause, dramatic effect, and side-eye precision.

Birdie added:

"And don't act like we don't know what y'all did to the hair salon on 25th.

You called it a fire hazard and turned it into a poke bowl bar."

By the time they got to Number 7, "Y'all paved over our history and replaced it with fro-yo and regret", the audience was clapping.

Even the interns were nodding.

"This building taught kids how to speak, dance, march, and register to vote.

And now you want to bulldoze it for a yoga studio with a dog spa?"

Somebody in the back yelled:

"Them dogs can stretch outside like the rest of us!"

Birdie raised her fist.

"We demand a city council meeting, a city hearing, and a folding chair for my sciatica right now!"

The crowd erupted.

The developer tried to regain control.

"We can talk offline if,"

Birdie raised Clarice.

"You'll talk right now, sweetheart.

We've got nowhere to be but the voting booth."

"I told you," She muttered, pouring Uncle Melvin's Private Reserve into a to-go cup.

"Here comes the good stuff."

"Oh, we 'bout to raise the roof now," Birdie said, eyes twinkling.

By the end of the night:

- The council tabled the project.
- The mayor asked for a one-on-one with Mama Lo.
- Birdie got invited to teach a seniors-only poker class at the new rec center.

Which, pending city funding, would be renamed:

The Birdie & Lo Legacy Lounge.

They danced. They chanted, they side-eyed every developer within ten miles, and by sunset, the protest was trending.

Gwen uploaded it to TikTok.

Dee-Dee emailed it to city council.

Zora-Lee was already writing the theme poem; Birdie waved her cane like a magic wand.

"See that? Still got the moves and the message."

Mama Lo nodded.

"That was holy. You did good, sis."

Birdie smiled.

"We did better than good.

We did grown-ass woman excellent."

GROWN ASS HAIKU – BY ZORA-LEE

Pantyhose protest
Wrinkled fists and righteous fire
We still kickin' ass

Eleven

SUNDRESSES, SUSPICION, AND MORE SHENANIGANS

Two Bougie Brunch Crashers & One Movement They Didn't Mean to Start, Starring Zora-Lee and Gwen.

Okay, y'all not gonna believe this one, Zora-Lee giggled, "Gwen and I damn near started a cult."

Mama Lo raised an eyebrow.

"Start from the beginning before I revoke your cocktail privileges."

Zora-Lee took a deep breath.

"It started with a coupon."

"It always starts with a coupon," Gwen cut in.

They'd seen it online, Vision Board Brunch: *Mimosas, Motivation & Millionaire Mindsets*, with a buy-one-get-one-free special.

Neither Zora-Lee nor Gwen had bothered to read the fine print.

All they knew was it came with bottomless Bellinis and a buffet.

"We walked in wearing sundresses and sandals," Gwen said.

"Meanwhile, these women were in blazers and TED Talk heels."

Zora-Lee nodded.

"And everybody had ring lights and planners with quotes like 'Be Her Now' on the covers."

Birdie leaned forward.

"Y'all stayed?"

Gwen grinned.

"Baby, we stayed! Walked in like we arrived for our own tribute concert."

The maître d' froze.

"Oh! Ladies! You're… early."

"We are?" Gwen blinked.

"Yes, the keynote brunch speakers," he whispered to the staff.

"We weren't expecting you for another twenty minutes."

Zora-Lee opened her mouth to correct him.

Gwen stepped in first.

"We decided to bless y'all ahead of schedule."

"Then," Zora-Lee added,

"Someone whispers to us, 'You're the surprise guests, right?' And Gwen goes…"

"'Damn right we are.'"

The room fell out.

"Y'all posed as the speakers?" Dee-Dee wheezed.

Fifteen minutes later, "Someone walked us in, and we had the nerve to sit at the front table and nod real serious," said Gwen.

They were seated, sipping mimosas and being stared at with reverence.

Gwen scanned the room, leaned in, and whispered,

"We are currently the Beyoncé and Solange of this garden patio."

Zora-Lee whispered back,

"What do they think we're speaking about?"

Just then, a woman at the next table leaned over, starry-eyed:

"We loved your last podcast episode, *Woke, Wiser & Moisturized*.

The line about peace and pedicures? Changed my life."

Gwen nodded solemnly.

"Mmm. That was a tough one.

Self-care doesn't always smell like lavender."

Zora-Lee added,

"Or as I said in the bonus episode: 'Forgiveness starts in your arches.'

That's why I wear good shoes to break generational trauma."

The woman burst into tears.

And asked for a selfie.

The gathering applauded.

Actual applause.

"By the time they handed us the mic, we had names, backstories, and fake Instagram handles," Gwen said proudly.

Zora-Lee picked up:

"I told them I was an expert in spiritual reclamation through melodic journaling."

"And I was a sensuality coach for burnout recovery," Gwen added.

"I almost started crying listening to myself."

She continued,

"Sisters, before you pour into others, check your pitcher.

If it's cracked, patch it with prayer and pressed powder."

Mama Lo hollered.

"Too much!"

"I told them to moan their way through fear," Gwen said.

Birdie just shook her head.

"And I made them write poems to their inner thighs," Zora-Lee chimed in.

Dee-Dee threw her napkin.

"I'm done!"

"I said, 'When's the last time you thanked your knees for carrying you through betrayal?'

And baby, they stood up and clapped!"

The women were hysterical with laughter. Gwen wiped her eyes.

Zora-Lee stood, slow and dramatic:

"If your peace can't be found," she said, "check the group chat.

Sometimes your chaos is saved under a contact name."

The room shouted,

"YAAASSSS!"

"Then this one woman comes up to us afterward," Gwen said,

"And says, 'I've never felt more seen.'"

But not everyone was convinced.

From across the room, a sharply dressed woman in a tangerine wrap dress narrowed her eyes.

She leaned toward a waiter and whispered,

"That ain't no damn podcast host. I saw the tall one at Target buying batteries."

The waiter shrugged.

"At Target? Well, she is inspiring. And her skin is phenomenal."

Before the woman could say another word, Zora-Lee caught her eye, raised her glass, and mouthed:

"Stay hydrated."

The woman blinked… then raised her glass right back.

And still took a selfie.

Back at their table, Gwen opened the brunch menu and nearly choked on her mimosa.

"Oh. My. God."

They had renamed the menu in real time:

BRUNCH WITH THE VISIONARIES

featuring Gwen & Zora-Lee

- **The Soft Reboot:** Peach cinnamon French toast with bourbon whipped cream
- **Emotional Support Greens:** Collard & kale fusion with affirmation vinaigrette
- **Trust No Man Benedict:** Poached eggs on a "toasted boundary" biscuit

- **The Legacy Plate:** Fried catfish, yams, and 'mind your business' slaw
- **#WokeWiserMoisturized Mimosa Flight:** Champagne, hibiscus, and a dash of healing

"Girl..." Zora-Lee whispered.

"We done turned Sunday brunch into a spiritual retreat."

"And I look good on this menu font," Gwen added.

"Helvetica has been waiting for me."

An hour and two gift bags later, they made it back to the car.

"Did we just start a movement?" Gwen asked, buckling her seatbelt.

Zora-Lee checked her phone.

"Someone just invited us to keynote a virtual summit on soul alignment and ankle strength."

Gwen grinned.

"I'll go if they serve the Emotional Support Greens."

Zora-Lee leaned back in her seat.

"Same dresses?"

Gwen winked.

"Same foolishness."

"We gave out hugs and left before the real speakers showed up," Zora-Lee added.

Mama Lo stood up and raised her glass.

"To fake it 'til you brunch it!"

All glasses clinked again, breathless from laughter.

GROWN ASS HAIKU – BY ZORA-LEE

Sundress, bold lip gloss
Sometimes, the best truth is jazz
And a damn good lie

JAZZ

CHAPTER
Twelve

TWO TICKETS TO FOOLISHNESS

Dressed Like Trouble at a Tuesday Matinee
Starring Dee-Dee & Gwen

The record had just flipped to the B-side, the Private Reserve was in full effect, and Miss Birdie was fanning herself like someone's auntie on revival Sunday.

Mama Lo leaned forward and topped off everyone's glass.

"Alright now, anybody else got somethin' foolish to share before I top off this reserve?"

Dee-Dee didn't even raise her hand. She just leaned back, eyes half-closed like she was about to deliver a testimony.

"Ohhhh honey. Gwen, you remember that matinee?"

Gwen side-eyed her, already grinning.

"Lawd. Don't start, Dee-Dee."

"Too late," Dee-Dee grinned.

"We telling it now. Gurl, y'all remember that time we got mistaken for guest speakers at the indie film panel?"

Zora-Lee perked up, notepad at the ready.

"Please start."

Dee-Dee clapped her hands once.

"Alright then. But don't say I didn't warn y'all, this one's got Sista Gwen's mistaken identity again, a rogue boa, and a clean kitchen exit."

It all started because Dee-Dee wanted popcorn.

Not regular popcorn.

Not the microwave kind.

The real kind.

With salt, butter, and the drama of a movie theater she didn't have to clean.

So, she sent out an S.O.S:

"I'm overdressed for errands and underwhelmed by life," she texted Gwen.

"Meet me at the Majestic. Matinee. I wanna be stared at. Put on something extra. We going to the artsy theater and I wanna look like trouble."

Gwen replied with one photo: a vintage black fur and a pair of red stilettos.

Caption: "Born for the spotlight."

Dee-Dee had a Groupon for a Tuesday afternoon matinee. Gwen had the afternoon off.

"It's some artsy independent film," Dee-Dee said.

"Probably got subtitles and somebody crying in a wheat field. But it's at that bougie theater with the good popcorn and cocktails."

Gwen had one rule:

"If I gotta read a movie, I need rum."

So off they went. Sunglasses on, lipstick fresh, and both of them wearing flowy, dramatic outfits that screamed,

Yes, we are somebody!

Dee-Dee wore her 'Educated AF' rhinestone sweatshirt under a tailored blazer, a skirt with a too-high slit, dark glasses, and a dramatic scarf.

Gwen wore cat-eye frames, red lipstick, and vintage earrings that could double as serving trays. Her wrap-coat took a full five seconds to settle every time she moved.

The moment they stepped into the lobby, late, everything slowed.

Scarves swished. Coats fluttered. Perfume lingered.

The ushers wore berets. Every film had a post-screening Q&A nobody understood.

The college volunteers at the box office blinked.

"Uh... are you two here for the screening?"

Gwen leaned in with her raspy smile.

"Baby, we are the screening."

A woman gasped.

"Oh my God! You're here!"

Dee-Dee blinked.

"In the living flesh."

The real mistake happened when the festival director walked by and gasped.

"Oh my God. You made it! The filmmakers from L.A.!"

Dee-Dee and Gwen exchanged glances. Squinted. Smiled.

"We wouldn't miss it," Gwen purred.

Turns out the festival's keynote speakers, a duo of radical feminist performance artists named Freedom & Fern, had missed their flight.

And somehow, someone looked at Dee-Dee and Gwen and thought,

That's them.

Before they could protest, they were swept into a VIP lounge, handed espresso, introduced to several confused white men in scarves, and given name tags:

Freedom and Fern.

Gwen, naturally, chose Fern.

"It sounds like a woman who waters her own damn plants," she said.

"And I look like I liberate spaces," Dee-Dee added.

"Fine. I'm Freedom."

The screening was... something foreign.

French? Maybe silent?

They didn't know what it was about, but they nodded and clapped in the right places.

Then came the announcement:

"Please welcome the filmmakers of *La Femme et l'Oiseau,* Fern and Freedom!"

A spotlight hit them.

They were led onto the stage.

Lights. Applause.

A sea of white women in linen.

"Say something inspiring," Gwen whispered.

"I got this," Dee-Dee whispered back.

She walked up like she was on the Sundance jury.

"Thank you," she said into the mic, slow and deep, like a grown woman who once dated a jazz pianist with no car.

"Sisters… and allies. Today we gather not to perform, but to reclaim."

Applause.

Gwen grabbed the mic:

"We reclaim joy. We reclaim rage. We reclaim… leisurewear."

The crowd erupted.

It snowballed.

Dee-Dee took the mic again:

"This film is… about duality.

About being too much and not enough.

About birds. Obviously.

And about the pressure Black women face to fly gracefully, even when their wings are tired or glued on with discount lashes."

They spoke for twenty minutes, about sisterhood, ancestral wisdom, silence, and wigs with structure.

Then came the Q&A.

"What is the greatest act of feminist resistance you've ever done?"

Dee-Dee:

"I refused to bring sweet potato pie to Thanksgiving after my cousin voted wrong."

Gwen:

"And I once left a man mid-date because he said Aretha was 'overrated.'"

"What was your favorite location to shoot?"

Gwen:

"The alley behind a soul food spot in Memphis. Real energy there."

"What camera did you use?"

Dee-Dee:

"The one with the lens."

"Did you mean for the color palette to symbolize oppression and rebirth?"

In unison:

"Yes!"

Back at Mama Lo's, the women were howling.

"Girl, we walked in twenty minutes late," Dee-Dee laughed.

"And left with a standing ovation."

"I still got that free tote bag," Gwen said.

"It holds all my mail and my petty."

Mama Lo shook her head, wheezing.

"Y'all are dangerous with an open door and a strong cocktail."

"The host saw two fine-ass Black women with flair walking in and just assumed we were somebody," Gwen said.

"And we weren't about to let them down."

Moral of the story? Dee-Dee raised her glass.

"If you can't find the spotlight…"

Gwen raised hers:

"Make your own damn stage."

In unison.

Miss Birdie raised her cane.

"Did y'all ever tell them the truth?"

Well… it was all going great, until he walked in.

A smooth-talking man in a turtleneck and trouble-colored slacks.

He squinted.

"Gwen… Gwen? From the Harlem jazz nights? Is that really you?"

The audience turned.

Gwen took a beat.

Then smiled wide:

"Sure is, baby. And if you'd returned my vinyl like I asked, maybe this film wouldn't be so angry."

The room howled.

"So y'all didn't get busted?" Zora-Lee asked.

"Nah," Dee-Dee shrugged.

"We took the gift baskets and left through the kitchen."

"They gave us an award," Gwen said, sipping her drink.

"It's in my living room next to the fake fern."

Mama Lo wheezed.

"Y'all ain't right!"

"Nope," Dee-Dee said.

"But we are memorable."

Birdie hollered.

"Y'all ain't even known what the movie was about!"

Gwen nodded.

"We should probably have Googled what the movie was about."

Dee-Dee snorted.

"Next time, I want a speaking fee."

Gwen grinned.

"Next time, I want a film credit."

They paused.

Then in unison:

"Same outfits?"

"Same foolishness."

GROWN ASS HAIKU – BY ZORA-LEE

Recognized as stars
Two legends, one wild story
Truth left in the seats.

The women raised their glasses.
   "To art. To performance.
   To never wasting a good lie when the moment calls."

JAZZ

Thirteen

IT'S THAT TIME

Well, ladies, Mama Lo said, stretching and eyeing the clock. "It's gettin' to be that time. You know what they say…"

She paused and took a dramatic sip from her glass.

"You ain't got to go home, but you got to get the hell up outta here. I got to lay me and Uncle Melvin down now."

The room broke into laughter.

Birdie waved her cane. "Speak for yourself, Lo. I done pulled my bra off. That's a contract. I am officially here for the night."

Zora-Lee slid farther down into her cushion. "I got some things to whisper to Uncle Melvin, too. He got me warm from the inside out."

Gwen raised her glass. "Don't whisper too loud, child. That Reserve got ears."

Dee-Dee leaned back, one sock off, one eyelash hanging on. "Y'all ever notice the more we sip, the more we testify?"

Mama Lo grinned. "That's the spirit talking, baby. Or the spirits."

Everyone laughed, but the energy had shifted, just a touch. The kind of hush that comes when the last song is playing and nobody really wants to leave.

Zora-Lee sat up and picked up her notebook, fingers brushing over the worn cover like it was velvet.

"I wrote something," she said.

The others settled in, quiet and ready, the glow of candlelight flickering against half-empty glasses and full hearts.

Zora-Lee took a deep breath, then opened her book.

"THE FINAL LINE" – BY ZORA-LEE

> If this is the last toast,
> Let it taste like truth.
> Aged in love,
> Sipped in sisterhood.
> Let the silence mean we're full,
> Not that we're finished.
> Let the tears mean we lived.
> Let the laughter mean we stayed.
> If this is the final line,
> Let it lead to more.
> Let it echo.
> Let it echo.
> Let it echo.

She closed her book.

Silence.

Then Gwen hollered, "Somebody put Aretha on!"

"Yass, to the Queen!" they all shouted back.

Zora-Lee wiped her cheek and raised her glass.

"To Black women stories. To thunder and lullabies."

"To stretch marks and unfinished poems!" Dee-Dee added.

"To lunch and bail money," Birdie toasted, grinning wide.

"To us," Mama Lo said, softly but steady.

The final clink of glasses felt like a benediction.

Same time.

Same bottles.

More hugs all around.

Same beautiful, messy, magical selves.

As Rea-Rea was winding down, Zora-Lee took a deep breath.

"But you know what? I'm learning. I used to think I had to shrink for people to love me. But now? I take up space. I take up pages."

Silence fell. Not out of shock, but reverence.

Zora-Lee exhaled and closed the book.

Birdie dabbed her eyes. "Now that's what I call a testimony."

Dee-Dee stood and raised her glass. "To the baby of the bunch. The poet. The woman who keeps us honest."

Gwen whispered, "She gave us goosebumps and giggles. My mascara ain't waterproof, dammit."

Mama Lo walked over and kissed the top of Zora-Lee's head. "You ain't the baby no more. You're the bard now."

Zora-Lee smiled through the shimmer in her eyes. "I love y'all. Even when you roast me."

"Oh, honey," Gwen said, clinking glasses, "that's just flavoring. Makes the story stick."

GROWN ASS HAIKU – BY ZORA-LEE

I bloomed in the shade
Grew wild under watchful eyes
Still learning to shine

The room hummed with a warmth that settled deep. This was more than a gathering, remember, it was a passing of soul, sip by sip.

Zora-Lee stretched her legs out on the floor; toes pointed like she was trying to find center.

"I used to think y'all were just glamorous chaos in heels," she said, grinning. "Now I realize you're glamorous chaos with purpose."

Dee-Dee leaned over. "You say that now, but we still remember the candle incident."

Zora-Lee gasped. "That was not my fault! That man said he liked ambience."

"You lit seven candles," Gwen deadpanned. "And forgot about the one under your wig."

"I was setting a mood! And my locs hadn't locked yet," Zora said, laughing so hard she slapped her own thigh.

Birdie wheezed. "Girl, you had a whole halo of fire and didn't even know it! Looked like a Pentecostal phoenix."

"Thank God for your satin bonnet," Mama Lo added, wiping tears. "Only thing that saved your edges, and those baby locs."

Zora-Lee buried her face in a pillow, still howling. "Okay, okay, I get it. I was young and flammable."

Dee-Dee lifted her glass. "To fire safety and bad dates."

"And to poems," Zora-Lee said, pulling her book back out, "because y'all been my fire too. You burned away the bullshit and made space for what matters."

She flipped to a marked page and took a deep breath.

Gwen looked up. "Girl, you got another one?"

"Yup," Zora-Lee smiled.

"WHAT CATCHES FIRE" – BY ZORA-LEE

> I used to beg for sparks,
> tiny flickers of maybe.
> Tried to build bonfires
> out of borrowed matches
> and gaslighting smiles.
> But then,
> Y'all showed up.

With candles and cackles,
gasoline truths,
and fans full of fight.
You didn't rescue me.
You re-lit me.
And now
everything I touch
catches fire.

When she finished, nobody moved for a full five seconds.

Then Dee-Dee whispered, "Girl. That's the poem you send to your future self."

Mama Lo was already refilling glasses like it was a sacred rite.

"You lit now, baby," Gwen said. "You might still be the baby, but that flame? That's woman-grown."

Birdie pointed her cane. "Tell 'em again with your chest."

Zora-Lee stood and raised her glass one more time.

"To stories. To slip-ups. To satin bonnets and smoke alarms. I love y'all."

They clinked.

The room sparkled with that glow that only comes when the youngest speaks like an old soul, and every grown-ass woman in the room sees themselves in her.

GROWN ASS HAIKU – BY ZORA-LEE

I learned in moonlight
How to glow without permission
Dark made me divine

JAZZ

CHAPTER
Fourteen

TRUTH BE TOLD

A Performance Poem That Held Them All – by Zora-Lee

The room was soft now, the fire had crackled down to embers, glasses sat half-full or completely abandoned, and the air buzzed with a quiet afterglow.

They'd laughed themselves hoarse, cried just a little more, and clutched memories like satin robes,

Them, and the robes, worn but still elegant.

The evening had crossed into that sacred pocket of time. It was the hour when the night loosened its grip and the room exhaled; no rushing, no performing, just women settling into themselves.

Zora-Lee now half-on, half-off the throw pillow now spooning it like a sweet memory.

Gwen's leopard-print heels were off, looking like they wanted to run away while she was flexing her toes.

Miss Birdie was, well, just looking at Uncle Melvin's Private Reserve like it had something more to say.

And Dee-Dee was just trying to keep her head up.

Zora-Lee stood up slowly.

"It's the last one… for tonight."
Sweat shimmered on her brow from another rogue hot flash,
but she didn't bother wiping it.
Her dreadlocks framed her face like living lines of a poem still being written.
The others watched her with the pride of women who had been there,
been her,
and now simply held space for her to shine.
She didn't announce it.
No longer needed to.
She just… began.

ZORA-LEE'S FINAL POEM (MAYBE)

I come from the hips of women
who carried joy like groceries
and pain like pocketbooks
they refused to put down.
From Sunday hats and side-eyes,
from lace gloves and kitchen grease,
from laughter that could resurrect a room.
I come from good wigs,
bad knees,
and stories soaked in gin, gossip, and God.
I come from them.
These women.
These queens in curlers and cackles.
They held me when I was shapeless.
Taught me to dance before I could doubt.
Fed me greens, wisdom, and moonshine truth.
Taught me to say "Woobaby!"
when life hit too hard.

Taught me to sip, slap, pray, and proceed.
Taught me that beauty don't expire,
it just deepens like a blues song.
Tonight, I watch them laugh
in leopard prints and legacy
and I see the woman I will one day be.
So I write this line in lipstick:
I will remember you.
I will remember this.
And I will tell it all… beautifully.

Zora-Lee exhaled, and for a long second, the room was utterly still.
Then,
"Woobaby," Mama Lo whispered, blinking slowly.
Birdie clapped once.
"That girl don't miss."
Gwen nodded, her voice raspy.
"That was the gospel."
Dee-Dee stood, raised her glass, and declared,
"To Zora-Lee. The poet. No more baby. And the grown-ass woman she has become."
They all stood with her.
They didn't speak for a long while.
Didn't need to.
The silence was sacred.
A kind of holy stillness that only comes when Black women gather,
tell the truth,
and leave nothing behind.
The night was almost over.
But the flame?
Still burned, no more stories tonight, only full hearts, warm rooms, and a promise:
They would be back next week.

More hugs all around.
Same time. Same bottles.
Same beautiful, messy, and magical selves.

78

GROWN ASS HAIKU – BY ZORA-LEE

They laughed me alive
Named me with their ancient breath
I became their song

Cousin Tina's Return

BANG! BANG! BANG!

The door shook like it owed someone money, Birdie yelped and grabbed Clarice so quickly she almost knocked over Uncle Melvin's Reserve.

Zora-Lee, sunk deep in that memory foam pillow, looked like a woman wrestling in slow motion, half-asleep, half-suffocating, and all confused.

Gwen still had her heels in hand, but now they were weapons, pointed, ready, and aimed like stilettos in a knife fight.

Mama Lo didn't flinch. She just closed her eyes real slow, like a woman who already knew exactly who was behind the chaos.

She muttered, "Lord, give me strength… or a fire escape."

Dee-Dee glanced at her, eyebrows raised, mouthing, "WTF?" before crossing the room like a bouncer on a mission.

She checked the peephole, turned back to Lo, and hissed, "You invited her?!"

Lo didn't answer.

SLAM!

The door swung open so hard the candles flickered.

And there she was.

Cousin Tina.

She stood in the doorway like she was waiting for applause.

When nobody offered it, she cleared her throat, softer this time.

"Y'all still on that grown woman sermon circle vibe? Don't mind me, I just came for the leftovers and maybe a little forgiveness."

She looked around the room.

Nobody moved.

Leopard leggings.

Off-the-shoulder sequined sweatshirt that read "Blessed but Petty."

Big hoop earrings. Bigger energy.

And a smile like she had news nobody wanted to hear.

She bounced from foot to foot, like she was deciding whether to flirt or fight.

"Cousin Lo!" she hollered, stepping right past Dee-Dee without making eye contact.

"Damn, y'all act like I'm the repo man or the ghost of bad decisions."

Mama Lo finally gestured toward the empty ottoman.

"Sit your tail down before Birdie uses that cane for crowd control."

Tina shuffled over and sat, looking at the furniture like it owed her rent, legs crossed, back straight, mouth almost closed.

Birdie, arms folded, muttered,

"We'll see how long this lasts."

The room exhaled. Not relaxed. Just… adjusting.

The way women do when someone you love keeps barging in through the wrong door,

but you still keep unlocking it.

Mama Lo stood up slowly and stretched.

"Alright. Coffee it is. Something's gotta balance out this whiskey and regret."

She padded off to the kitchen in her house shoes, mumbling something about

"dark roast and discernment."

Gwen wandered to the record player and slid a new vinyl from its sleeve.

"Let's soften this vibe before someone says something that makes me call my therapist again."

She dropped the needle on a mellow track, soft jazz with just enough bass to stir a memory.

Birdie, still perched like a queen with a grudge, pulled a sugar packet from the tray and poured it into her glass instead of her coffee.

"This is me being sweet," she said without smiling.

Zora-Lee tucked her feet underneath her and curled into herself, eyes half-closed, breath deep.

She wasn't sleeping, she was holding the moment, saving it for a poem she hadn't written yet.

Dee-Dee, arms crossed, didn't say a word.

Just watched Tina like she was daring her to make one wrong move.

"Whew. If I knew happy hour turned into a silent retreat, I'da stayed home with my Pinot and problems."

Zora-Lee finally sat up.

"We were chillin', not sleepin'. There's a difference."

Birdie narrowed her eyes.

"Depends on who just walked in."

Mama Lo, eyes narrow, asked,

"You here for a reason, or just to stir the gumbo?"

Tina fanned herself dramatically.

"Ooooh. I feel the tension. What's the theme tonight? Truth or resentment?"

Gwen muttered,

"It was peace… until now."

"Y'all remember the last time she said she was just gonna 'drop in for a sec'? We ended up in a group text with her ex, her landlord, and a numerologist named Jermaine."

"I thought Jermaine had insight!" Tina shot back.

Zora-Lee leaned in, sipping slowly.

"Sis, you asked a complete stranger if Mercury in retrograde was the reason you kept dating broke men."

"Okay, that might've been a reach," Tina said, then added, "but he said maybe."

Everyone groaned.

Dee-Dee slid a coaster across the coffee table toward her.

"Tina. We love you. We do. But tonight ain't about therapy, apologies, or charting your love life by the moon."

Tina sat quietly for a beat, her coffee warming her hands but not quite her face.

"If I hear one more story that starts with, 'So I met this man,' I'm personally escorting you to the nearest Unbothered Boot Camp."

Tina smirked.

"What if it starts with, 'So I left this man,'?"

Dee-Dee blinked, then exhaled dramatically.

"Okay. Okay, that's different."

Laughter rippled.

Birdie clinked her glass against Tina's without comment, a silent offer of 'don't screw it up.'

Gwen leaned back and hummed the first line of "Love and Happiness."

Zora-Lee closed her eyes, letting the night settle in her bones.

Mama Lo stood slowly, towering not in height but in presence.

"Here's to the ones who show up raggedy, real, and right on time."

She lifted her mug high.

"To the ones who come back, even if they left wrong."

"To the ones who try, fail, try again, and still bring a damn casserole."

"And to all of us, for not locking the door."

The women raised their glasses in a soft clatter of communion.

Zora-Lee pulled a small scrap of paper from her pocket.

Tina slowly put her other hand up.

"I know! I know. I'm just here to chill. I promise."

Birdie tilted her head.

"So no updates on the dude with the neck tattoo who borrowed your blender and never brought it back?"

"Birdie!" Tina whined,

now holding up both hands like she was being frisked.

"Look, I ain't gonna lie. I didn't wanna go home yet. Place is too quiet. Feels like I'm waiting for a phone call that ain't comin'… and a man who already left. And, I'm tired, y'all. Not just 'I had a day' tired. I'm like… 'every decision I ever made is catching up to me' tired."

Silence fell, not because they were stunned, but because that was honest.

Zora-Lee's face softened.

"That's real."

Dee-Dee rolled her eyes.

"Again?"

Tina ignored the jab.

"And y'all know I been thinkin'. Maybe I could… you know… be part of the club?"

You could've heard a lip gloss cap click.

"Like, officially?" Zora-Lee asked.

Birdie sipped her drink without breaking eye contact.

"Define 'be part of the club.'"

Tina perked up.

"Like… be in the circle. Get a chair. A glass. One of those cute little poems at the end."

She shrugged, almost embarrassed.

"It's just, sometimes I leave places too soon. Sometimes I stay too long. I don't always know how to land in the middle. But y'all? This feels like... the middle I've been trying to find."

Mama Lo said,

"Then stop knocking like the police and start showing up like somebody who belongs."

Gwen chuckled without humor.

"Tina, baby. We love you. But you don't bring a poem, you bring a hurricane."

Dee-Dee sighed.

"And no offense, but if we gotta hear one more 'He don't love me, he broke, and he borrowed my car' story,"

"It was MY Nissan!" Tina shot back.

"We gon' put you on mute, baby," Dee-Dee finished.

Zora-Lee smirked.

"I got love for you, Tina. But this club? It ain't therapy, and it ain't a talent show."

Tina picked up a coaster, turned it in her hands, and tapped her foot politely to the music.

She looked like a kid who'd been told not to ask for anything in the store.

"So... y'all heard about,"

Every head turned.

"I mean... never mind. That's not my business."

Tina was trying her best.

Birdie snorted.

"Since when?! You are the Queen of Other People's Business!"

Tina giggled.

"I know, I know. I'm trying. Growth is hard."

Gwen raised an eyebrow.

"Growth has a five-minute expiration with you."

Tina sighed dramatically and sipped her coffee, which clearly wasn't strong enough for the effort it took to hold her tongue.

There was a pause.

A silence.

A beat.

Then, "Okay, but I have to tell y'all what happened to Tonya and that Jamaican mechanic with the gold teeth."

"Lawd, here she go," Dee-Dee muttered.

Tina launched into it anyway.

"So apparently, she caught him in her brand-new shower with her landlord, and the worst part? The shower wasn't even finished yet! She was still waiting on the tile to be sealed, and there they were, just,"

Mama Lo reappeared, coffee mug in hand, unimpressed.

"Tina."

"I know. I'm terrible."

Zora-Lee cracked a smile.

"No. You're just Tina."

"Exactly the problem," Dee-Dee muttered.

But then…

Laughter.

From Gwen.

Then Birdie.

Then Zora-Lee.

Even Dee-Dee broke, shaking her head as she chuckled.

"That poor shower. Hadn't even had its grout set and already got baptized in sin."

"To sin and sealant," Gwen toasted.

"To gossip that ain't useful but sure is funny," Mama Lo added.

Tina looked around the room, her voice smaller now.

"I'm trying, y'all. I just… I don't wanna go home yet."

Zora-Lee leaned over and placed her hand gently on Tina's.

"Then don't. Sit. Sip. Try again tomorrow."

Mama Lo nodded.

"You ain't gotta be perfect to be in this room. But you do have to be honest."

Tina smiled, tired, hopeful, a little cracked around the edges.

"Okay. I can do that."

Mama Lo walked over to Tina, looked her dead in the eyes.

"This circle holds space," Lo said.

"But it doesn't perform rescue missions. You want in? You gotta bring more than your drama. You gotta bring your truth. Not just the kind that sounds good with wine, but the kind that makes you sit in your own mess first."

Tina opened her mouth, then shut it.

Her lip trembled just slightly. Just once.

Then she nodded. Quietly.

"Let her stay tonight," Birdie said, cane clinking.

"But if she starts crying over that man with the busted grill and no job, I'm throwing her purse out the window."

"And if she says 'I just feel like y'all don't hear me', we are turning up the jazz and changing the topic," Gwen added.

Tina laughed softly, wiping the corner of her eye.

"Damn. Y'all are mean."

"No, baby. We're grown," Zora-Lee said, handing her a glass.

Dee-Dee looked at Tina, then muttered,

"One more toe outta line, and you're on ice duty for the next three parties."

"I'll bring crushed and cubed," Tina grinned.

From the hallway, someone's phone buzzed.

Birdie side-eyed it.

"If it's that same man who still owes you brunch and back rent, don't answer."

Tina picked it up, peeked at the screen, and slid it into her purse without a word.

"I'm good," she said.

Mama Lo nodded.

"That's a start."

The night exhaled.

Not ended, just paused.

Somewhere between grace and gossip,

they let one more woman sit at the table.
Same time. Same bottles. More hugs all around.
Same beautiful, messy, magical selves.

GROWN ASS HAIKU – BY ZORA-LEE

Showed up. Broke the peace.
Still made room for her teacup.
Sisterhood ain't neat.

JAZZ

CHAPTER
Sixteen

NOW I'M HUNGRY

With Recipes, Reminders, and One Steamy Story

The room had just begun to settle again, Mama Lo stretched her arms and cracked her neck.

"Alright y'all, we've cried, we confessed, we cussed a little, some more than others," she side-eyed Birdie. "But now…"

She looked toward the kitchen like it owed her an apology.

"Now I'm hungry."

Birdie didn't miss a beat.

"If there ain't no deviled eggs left, somebody's gonna be deviled tonight."

Gwen groaned, tossing a pillow aside.

"Don't start. Every time we eat late, I end up dreamin' my ex is smothered in gravy and forgiveness."

Zora-Lee, barely lifting her head from the pillow, mumbled,

"Mmm. Can we DoorDash deliverance?"

But Mama Lo was already headed toward the kitchen, dragging a silk scarf off her head like she was about to wrestle some greens.

"I made gumbo," she said.

"The good kind. Shrimp, crab, okra, sassafras, and enough heat to make your back sweat."

That got them up.

Dee-Dee peeked inside the pot and let out a moan.

"Lo, this smells like a second chance and a third mistake."

Zora-Lee gasped.

"Who taught you to cook like this?"

Mama Lo didn't turn around.

"My Aunt Ruthie. She believed in food as therapy and cayenne as punctuation."

Birdie nodded.

"That woman's cornbread made grown men confess affairs and propose in the same breath."

Mama Lo poured the gumbo into mismatched bowls like she was anointing them.

"Food is holy," she said.

"And so are we. Especially when it's late, and your heart's still chewing on the day."

Mama Lo took her seat like a queen returning to court, gumbo in hand, eyes warm.

"This right here," she said, "is why we never go to bed mad or hungry."

Birdie held up a spoon like a sermon.

"I once fixed a whole beef stew just to tell my ex I was over him. By the time the cornbread came out, he was crying and I was already texting his cousin."

Zora-Lee's eyes went wide.

"You didn't!"

"I did, baby. Sometimes the revenge is in the roux."

Dee-Dee grabbed a spoon.

"Let the church say,"

"AMEN and pass the hot sauce!" Birdie yelled, already reaching for it.

There it was again, laughter full and throaty. The kind that fills the cracks of everything they hadn't said yet.

"This tastes like memories and permission," Zora-Lee whispered.

"That's because it is," Mama Lo smiled.

Moments later, tongues now massaging lips…

Gwen opened the fridge, spotting a covered dish.

"Who made the peach cobbler?"

"I did," Dee-Dee announced, hands on her hips.

"From scratch. With a dash of nutmeg and a wink. I dropped it off earlier while it was still warm."

Birdie eyed her suspiciously.

"You sure you didn't just charm it out of somebody else's oven?"

Now, the group gathered again at the table, bowls in hand, cobbler waiting its turn.

Dee-Dee grinned.

"Why steal a recipe when you can steal the baker?"

Everyone hollered.

She leaned over the counter, suddenly smug.

"Y'all remember Nadine?"

Mama Lo raised an eyebrow.

"Short hair, tall attitude?"

"Uh huh," Dee-Dee nodded.

"She tasted my cobbler once. Just once. Next thing I know, she's 'droppin' by' every Sunday like I was runnin' a damn bakery and not a one-woman show."

Birdie cackled.

"What'd you do?"

"I served her seconds. And then…"

Dee-Dee let her voice drop low and lazy.

"Next thing I know, she's behind me, whisperin' somethin' sweet, and somehow, my apron's being pulled up over my head like it had other plans, and we ended up tangled in my kitchen blinds."

"Ma'am!" Gwen nearly spit out her gumbo.

Dee-Dee just sipped her drink, eyes twinkling.

"That cobbler was hot out the oven."

"This is why I take notes around y'all," Zora-Lee choked on her laugh.

Gwen added with a smirk,

"You ever notice how the best cooks got the best hips? We been seasoning and slow-roasting more than chicken for decades."

Digging into her peach cobbler, Gwen paused mid-bite.

"You ever notice how food tastes better when you don't give a damn?"

"Or when somebody's looking at you like you're the dessert?" Dee-Dee nodded, swirling her bourbon.

That got a round of, "Oooh!s and side-eyes.

Zora-Lee fanned herself with a napkin.

"This room needs a rating system."

"Girl, this room is the rating system," Gwen replied, popping another spoonful into her mouth.

Then Tina, who had been suspiciously quiet, licking cobbler crumbs from her spoon, spoke up:

"I once made shrimp and grits for a woman who swore she didn't even eat seafood. She left wearing one of my robes and my middle name."

The table exploded.

Dee-Dee slapped the table.

"Not the middle name, Tina!"

Tina shrugged, smug.

"I had a whole breakfast playlist queued up and everything."

Birdie leaned over, eyes narrowed.

"What was the playlist called?"

Tina winked.

"Salt, Sugar, & Savory Sin."

"Y'all are outta control," Zora-Lee wheezed.

Mama Lo laughed so hard she had to wipe her eyes.

"This right here? This is how we survive. We stir, we season, and we spill just enough to keep it interesting."

Then she leaned back, eyes softening.

"My Aunt Ruthie used to say, 'The best recipes aren't written, they're whispered.' Passed down in between heartbreak and healing. You never just get the dish. You get the woman who made it, too."

A beat of silence. The kind that held weight without hurting.

Zora-Lee set her bowl down.

"I want to learn. Not just what y'all make, but how to carry what y'all carry."

Mama Lo nodded.

"Then you start in the kitchen. You stir with your whole wrist, your whole back, your whole story."

Birdie added,

"And don't you ever apologize for how spicy your truth is. If it's too hot, they can blow on it."

Laughter returned, bubbling up like the gumbo. Full, hearty, needed.

Gwen raised her glass again.

"To the women who cooked before us. Who stirred with soul, danced in the kitchen, and told the truth with every bite."

They toasted.

"To the ones who fed us body and spirit."

"To food that lingers longer than any man ever did."

"To peach cobbler and pulled aprons."

And as the dishes emptied and the wine ran low, a slow song slid through the speakers.

Zora-Lee stood, barefoot, bowl still in hand.

"We've got one more chapter in us tonight."

And just like that… hips began to sway again.

GROWN ASS HAIKU

They ate like queens and survivors.

Like women who knew hunger in all its forms, some
spiritual, some sensual,
all deserving of seconds.

94

CHAPTER
Seventeen

ONE MORE SONG, ONE MORE SIP

*(Now with House Shoes, Low Lighting, and a Warning Label for
Hips Over Forty)*

The clock didn't matter anymore, they'd toasted a dozen toasts, passed around stories like serving trays, and slipped into that sacred sliver of night when time slowed and the truth got bolder.

Zora-Lee was the first to rise.

Her hair a little flatter, eyes glassier, but her voice still steady.

"Put on something with bass, Gwen. My spirit just told my feet to wake up."

Mama Lo chuckled from her chair.

"If your spirit told your feet anything, it should be, 'Stretch first.'"

Dee-Dee stood too, wobbling slightly, arms up.

"Ain't no bedtime in this sisterhood. Not 'til the floor creaks and somebody's wig hits the lamp."

Gwen gave the record player a knowing look, fingers hovering before she chose the cut, one of those deep, syrupy grooves that could melt waistlines and raise eyebrows.

The needle dropped.

Boom.

Bass.

And just like that, the living room turned into a revival.

Miss Birdie kicked off her shoes with a grunt and stood with help from Clarice.

"Let me tell y'all right now," she warned, already swaying,

"if I throw this hip out, somebody call my chiropractor and my manicurist. One of 'em can fix it, the other can lie about it."

The beat hit again.

Zora-Lee spun once, awkward but determined.

Dee-Dee dropped it low then immediately hollered,

"OHHH my quads! Why didn't nobody warn me that 50 is a full-body sport?!"

Mama Lo, still seated, began doing the Electric Slide with just her arms and her martini.

"I'm participating from the waist up," she declared.

"The rest of me has clocked out."

Tina, somehow already barefoot, was twirling with a scarf like she'd just discovered interpretive dance.

"You're doing a lot," Birdie muttered.

"That's right," Tina grinned. "I am a lot. I'm a whole lot and a half."

Then came the moment.

The music slowed. It shifted.

Something silky and familiar slipped through the speakers, one of those grown songs.

The kind that made you call people you shouldn't

and feel things you weren't ready for.

Everyone froze.

Then Gwen said softly,

"Y'all remember this one?"

Zora-Lee smiled.

"My mama used to hum it while cooking greens."

Dee-Dee sighed.

"My ex used to play it trying to be sexy. He wasn't."

Birdie closed her eyes, letting the first few bars settle into her shoulders.

"This was my 'put on lipstick and make bad decisions' anthem."

They moved together now.

Not choreographed, not cool, just real.

Arms swinging, hips creaking,

bodies remembering what joy felt like before it had to be justified.

They didn't dance for an audience.

They danced for their own release.

For their mothers and their missed chances.

For the hips that still worked and the knees that sometimes didn't.

For the memories stored in their spines

and the magic that was never meant to be quiet.

Laughter bubbled up again, wild, tearful, too full to hold in.

Zora-Lee tripped over Birdie's cane.

Birdie caught her.

"Don't go down, baby. You got more rhythm than floor space."

Mama Lo raised her glass from the couch.

"To every woman who ever left a dance floor too early because she didn't want to sweat out her hair."

Dee-Dee saluted her with a slice of leftover pound cake.

"To sweat, to joy, to whatever this move is I'm doing right now that feels like twerking but might actually be a cramp."

When the music faded, no one rushed to start another song.

The silence after a good song was almost holy.

Zora-Lee stayed seated, eyes soft.

"You ever feel like your body held a story too long? Like… it started to hum from the inside out?"

No one answered right away.

They didn't need to.

Then Gwen leaned forward, resting her chin in her hand.

"I told a man I loved him once," she said.

"Right after I found his other phone."

The room gasped.

Birdie clutched her pearls.

"Was it worth it?"

Gwen grinned.

"The lie or the phone bill?"

More laughter.

Mama Lo took a deep breath and said,

"My secret? I haven't cried since 1997. I tried once. Got as far as a tear duct. But I think the faucet broke. Or got welded shut after that whole mess with Roscoe and the courthouse."

Even Tina went quiet.

Birdie shook her head.

"I once faked a fall in church so I wouldn't have to sing with Sister Maybelle. She hit notes that made the angels wince."

Zora-Lee covered her mouth.

"Miss Birdie!"

"She was flat, baby. But her wigs were ambitious."

Dee-Dee rolled her eyes and sipped.

"Alright. Here's mine."

Everyone turned.

"I used to keep a 'Go Bag' for breakups," she said.

"Hair ties, mascara, and a bottle of prosecco."

Gwen blinked.

"That's not a confession, that's self-care."

"No," Dee-Dee smiled.

"The confession is that I used it twice… before breaking up. I just wanted to be ahead of the emotional mess."

They howled.

Mama Lo snapped,

"You had pre-game therapy?"

Dee-Dee nodded.

"Some folks hoard receipts. I hoard emotional exit plans."

Zora-Lee whispered,

"I love us."

Then came the hush.

Not silence, just that soft drift of breath

when women realize they're holding something tender together.

Mama Lo looked around the room, eyes glistening, not from sadness, but from the heat of too much laughter and just enough release.

"I say we make it official," she said.

"No more rationing joy. Not for work, not for kids, not for damn church committees."

Birdie raised her glass.

"And definitely not for men with two phones."

"Or knees that pop like microwave popcorn," Gwen added.

"Or fear," Zora-Lee whispered. "Especially not that."

Dee-Dee set her drink down with purpose.

"So what's the plan?"

Mama Lo smiled.

"We keep showing up. We keep telling it, even when it's ugly. Even when it's loud. Even when it's brilliant and nobody's ready for it."

Tina chimed in,

"And we don't apologize for it, right?"

This time, no one laughed. They just nodded.

Agreement didn't always need applause.

They sat like that for a while.

Half-drunk. Fully alive.

The couch sighed under their weight.

The candles gave a last flicker.

The music hummed softly in the background,

a low current tying them to the world.

Birdie adjusted her hat.

"If someone don't make a club motto outta this, I swear I will."

Mama Lo leaned back and said,

"Baby, this whole night is the motto."

Now the couch had started to hold them like old church pews, deep-set and full of secrets.

Dee-Dee looked around and grinned.

"Alright. New rule. If there's one thing you ain't said out loud yet, now's the time to spill it."

Birdie raised a brow.

"Is this a confession circle or an emotional striptease?"

"Both," Gwen said, kicking off her heels again.

"And I better not be the only one taking somethin' off."

Zora-Lee giggled.

"Y'all are a mess."

Dee-Dee pointed her glass at her.

"You first."

Zora-Lee held up her hands.

"Okay, fine. One time, I faked an orgasm… just to get out of a second round of karaoke with my ex."

They roared.

"He kept singing Boyz II Men," she shrugged.

"It was survival."

Gwen wiped her eyes.

"Alright. I once walked into a revival with no drawers on because I forgot laundry day was Sunday and thought, 'The Lord knows my heart, and my hamper.'"

Lo gasped.

"That's the devil's work!"

"I was anointed in spirit. Just not in Spanx."

Birdie shook her head, chuckling.

"Y'all are amateurs. I once wrote anonymous letters to the church gossip with Bible verses about minding her own business."

Zora-Lee slapped the couch.

"You're the reason Sister Odell stopped speaking in tongues!"

Mama Lo stood and stretched, dramatically.

"Okay. Listen up. One more truth from each of us. But this time, make it the kind that's been riding your shoulders for too damn long."

Gwen groaned.

"You mean like real-real?"

"Real grown," Lo said.

Dee-Dee crossed her arms.

"Fine. I secretly hope one of my exes is stalking my glow-up. Just once, I want to post a thirst trap that leads to an apology."

Birdie nodded.

"I still wonder what my life would've looked like if I'd married Earl instead of entertaining that damn saxophone player."

"Those saxophone players. Just something about them hitting the right notes," Gwen said.

Zora-Lee's voice dropped.

"Sometimes I feel like I'm not wise enough to be sitting here with y'all."

Lo reached over, touched her hand.

"Baby, wisdom ain't about age. It's about receipts. And trust me, we've all got a purse full."

They sat back, warm from the laughter and truth.

Lo raised her glass, not high, just firm.

"No more rationing joy," she said.

"Not for jobs, not for respectability, not for hips that crack when we laugh too hard."

"Not for anyone who don't clap when we win," Dee-Dee added.

"Not even for grandkids that forget to call," Birdie said.

"Or bras that betray us mid-conversation," Zora-Lee grinned.

The women clinked their glasses with the kind of grin that comes when you know you earned your place at the table.

They tried to stand again but, they were still.

Breathing.

Holding onto one another like the floor might shift beneath them if they let go.

Birdie wiped her forehead with a napkin fished from her bra.

Gwen leaned her head on Mama Lo's shoulder.

Zora-Lee sat cross-legged, barefoot, humming softly like she was storing the night for later.

Tina whispered,

"Can we do this again? Like, real soon?"

Mama Lo answered for them all.

"We already are."

GROWN ASS HAIKU – BY ZORA-LEE

Joy behind closed doors
Secrets softened by candle
Laughter saves again

CHAPTER

Eighteen

THE FINAL LINE

(One Last Shot, One Legendary Night)

There was just enough left in Uncle Melvin's Private Reserve for one final sin, Mama Lo didn't ask. She poured.

A smooth slide across the table, like temptation in a bottle.

The liquid shimmered gold in the candlelight.

"One more for the memories," she said.

Birdie squinted.

"You been saying that since Chapter 3," then licked her lips.

"This memory's gonna need ice and alibis."

"Fine. One last one for real."

They each took their glasses,

a shared breath and a flicker of wild in every eye.

Dee-Dee raised her glass.

"To the nights we almost behaved."

Clink.

They didn't sip.

They savored.

Let it burn a little.

Let it baptize their tongues and wake up everything that had gone soft.

Then Dee-Dee did what she always did:

kicked the moment square in the behind.

"Alright, ladies," she said, standing and shimmying her shoulders.

"Let's end this right. Somebody queue the playlist before my hips forget how to flirt."

Zora-Lee grabbed her phone.

"Oh, I got something."

A beat dropped.

And just like that, the air changed.

Zora-Lee stood slowly, stretching like a cat in moonlight.

"Mmm… my body's talkin'," she said.

"Y'all hear that bass?"

Her hips already swaying, and the playlist kicked in.

A slow, pulsing groove, grown and knowing.

Shoes came off like confessions.

Birdie flung her red hat onto the couch with flair,

then peeled her red blazer off like she meant business.

Gwen slid her hoops back in.

Mama Lo adjusted her strapless bra with a smirk and said,

"If the girls stay in place, we stay on the floor."

Mama Lo untied her headwrap and let her silver curls bounce free.

Gwen rolled up her sleeves and cracked her knuckles like a woman ready for a soul revival.

The bass thumped. The beat slapped.

And the women?

Dee-Dee didn't wait for permission.

She started a body roll so smooth it should've come with a warning label.

They danced.

Dancing like they had back in somebody's basement in '78.
Gwen screamed,
"You got, you got, you got what I need!"
She got low, not floor low,
but "enough to be illegal in three states" low.
Dancing-like knees weren't a factor, and joy had no curfew.
Birdie moved like slow fire, twirling Clarice and biting her lip.
Dancing like every hot flash was just extra glow.
Zora-Lee spun like the room belonged to her.
To old-school basslines and new reasons to live.
To stretch marks that mapped every lesson.
To thighs that thundered and arms that remembered the rhythm.
Mama Lo gave a full-body grind that made Dee-Dee shout,
"Alright now, Lo! Save some scandal for Volume Two!"
Even Tina, halfway through another warmed-up bowl of gumbo,
popped her hip and kept chewing.
The air was thick with heat and harmony.
Glasses half-full.
Bodies full of stories.
Shoulders glowing with sweat and survival.
They weren't just dancing, they were declaring.
Yes, I still got it.
Yes, I want joy I don't have to explain.
Yes, I look damn good barefoot in pearls and sweatpants.
Then the music slowed, but the sensual stayed.
The lights stayed low.
The mood stayed high.
Lo turned the record to something smoky and slow.
Dee-Dee pulled Zora-Lee into a two-step.
Birdie slow-danced with Clarice like a lover from the past.
Gwen swayed with her eyes closed, mouthing every lyric.
No one rushed to end it.
When the final note hung in the air, they collapsed, in chairs,
on cushions,

across each other like warm laundry.
Zora-Lee whispered,
"Same time next month?"
Lo smirked.
"Same bottles."
Dee-Dee, breathless, added,
"Same hips… if they recover."
Birdie raised one hand.
"More hugs. And no damn Spanx."
Gwen, hair wild, voice honeyed and hoarse, smiled wide.
"Same beautiful, messy, magical selves."
The room pulsed with afterglow.
No toast. No speech.
Just women who had danced themselves clean.
Sexy. Spent. Sacred.

GROWN ASS HAIKU – BY ZORA-LEE

Feet bare, hips honest
We danced past what held us down
Morning kissed our shine

"Club Rules, Wink, Wink"

A beautiful Grown Ass Woman contradiction
(Posted next to the bar. Etched in soul.)

1. **Come as you are.**
2. **Laugh from your belly.**
3. **Cry if you need, ugly, pretty, or in between.**
4. **Never apologize for a second plate, a second chance, or a second wind.**
5. **High heels are optional. Big feelings are not.**
6. **Say her name when she forgets it herself.**
7. **Leave the door cracked for the next woman.**
8. **Tell the truth, especially the funny version.**
9. **Dance like your knees don't know better.**
10. **And always, always:**
11. **Never let joy be rationed again.**

JAZZ

*

Epilogue

WHISPER

After the Music Fades
Just a gentle exhale to carry us into what's next...

The music was off, but the room still swayed, Soft as a secret, like it remembered every beat, every shout, every footstep that refused to apologize for joy.

Laced with lipstick, laughter, and that late-night afterglow that only the Grown Ass Women's Club can deliver, No grand goodbye.

Heels were scattered like confessions.

Glasses half-full, hearts overflowing.

Cushions held the shape of bodies that had leaned in, loved hard, and let go.

A lone candle flickered on the coffee table.

Zora-Lee was the last to move.

She crossed to the window barefoot, her fan drooping from her fingers,

makeup smudged into memory.

Outside, the street was quiet.

But inside?

The air still hummed with everything
they had dared to say, laugh, sing, and shake loose.
On the fridge, a note written in red lipstick on a napkin:
"Same time. Same bottles.
Bring your secrets and your sass."
Signed,
The Grown Ass Women's Club

Volume One: Closed.

But baby… the door is always open.

***Volume One: Mic dropped. Sealed with love, sweat, and lipstick.
Legacy rising.***
"Legacy"
(A soft, wise closer about what these stories truly mean)

These aren't just stories.
They're offerings.
Laughter passed down.
Wrinkles worn like medals.
Lipstick as war paint.
Secrets that bloomed into truth because someone
    was finally brave enough to say them out
    loud.
The Grown Ass Women's Club isn't just a book.
It's a mirror.
A legacy.
And a promise:
We don't whisper our names anymore.
We say them bold.
With bass.
And all the attitude we want!

JAZZ

www.ingramcontent.com/pod-product-compliance
Lightning Source LLC
Chambersburg PA
CBHW071444130726
47997CB00006B/2219